The Somme
INCLUDING ALSO **The Coward**

The Joseph M. Bruccoli Great War Series

EDITORIAL BOARD
Matthew J. Bruccoli, Series Editor
Hugh Cecil
Horst Kruse
Steven Trout

—◆—

"All that is needed to understand World War I in its philosophical and historical meaning is to examine barbed wire—a single strand will do—and to meditate on who made it, what it is for, why it is like it is." —JAMES DICKEY

The Somme

INCLUDING ALSO **The Coward**

A. D. Gristwood

PREFACE BY H. G. WELLS

New Introduction by Hugh Cecil

THE UNIVERSITY OF SOUTH CAROLINA PRESS

New material © 2006 University of South Carolina

Cloth edition published by Jonathan Cape, 1927
Paperback edition published by the University of South Carolina Press
in Columbia, South Carolina

Manufactured in the United States of America

15 14 13 12 11 10 09 08 07 06   10 9 8 7 6 5 4 3 2 1

Library of Congress Cataloging-in-Publication Data

Gristwood, A. D. (Arthur Donald), 1893–1933.
    The Somme, including also The coward / A. D. Gristwood ; preface
by H. G. Wells ; new Introduction by Hugh Cecil.
        p. cm. — (The Joseph M. Bruccoli Great War series)
    ISBN-13: 978-1-57003-648-4 (pbk : alk. paper)
    ISBN-10: 1-57003-648-9 (pbk : alk. paper)
    1. Somme, 1st Battle of the, France, 1916– Fiction. 2. World War,
1914–1918 —Fiction. I. Gristwood, A. D. (Arthur Donald), 1893–1933.
Coward. II. Title. III. Title: Somme.
    PR6013.R765S66 2006
    823'.912—dc22

                                                          2006019670

This book was printed on EcoBook Natural, a recycled paper with
50 percent postconsumer waste content.

Contents

Series Editor's Preface

The Joseph M. Bruccoli Great War Series republishes fiction and personal narratives—the demarcation is not always clear—from the belligerent nations of World War I. Formal military history is excluded. "The war to end all wars" generated a vast literature—much of it antiheroic and antiwar. The best books of the war convey a sense of betrayal, loss, and disillusionment. Many of them now qualify as forgotten books, although they were admired in their time. The intention of this series is to rescue once-influential books that have been long out of print.

The volumes are drawn from the Joseph M. Bruccoli Great War Collection in the Thomas Cooper Library, University of South Carolina.* This collection is named for a private in the AEF who was severely wounded on the Western Front. Joseph M. Bruccoli's medal has seven battle bars, and he claimed two more battles. He was not embittered by his war.

M.J.B

*The Joseph M. Bruccoli Great War Collection at the University of South Carolina: An Illustrated Catalogue, compiled by Elizabeth Sudduth (Columbia: University of South Carolina Press, 2005). See also The Joseph M. Bruccoli Great War Collection in the University of Virginia Library, compiled by Edmund Berkeley Jr. (Columbia: MJB, 1999).

Introduction

HUGH CECIL

The Somme, by Arthur Donald Gristwood, with its companion tale, *The Coward,* is one of the most disturbing works of fiction by a British veteran to come out of the Great War of 1914–18. The double novel was published in London by Jonathan Cape late in 1927, over a year before antiwar books became fashionable. Dark and comfortless, it serves as a reminder that the war could not only wreck a man's body, but his soul as well.

In the view of H. G. Wells, who wrote the original foreword, what singled out "Mr. Gristwood's unheroic tale" was "the relentless simplicity to recall things as they were," where most people "instinctively destroy the record of how miserable we were or how afraid we were."* Every schoolboy with a taste for soldiering should read it, Wells urged; for they were far more likely to find themselves following Gristwood's path, that of the ordinary foot soldier, than that of some heroic leader.

The Somme tells the story of a futile attack during the 1916 Somme campaign in which the central character, Tom Everitt, is wounded. His self-centered, uncourageous conduct in and out of the line is all too easy for readers to imagine their own might be like in similar circumstances. *The Coward* is about a soldier who commits an offense punishable by death in order to escape from the battlefield and who is haunted by fear of discovery and, later, by shame. Gristwood's main point in both stories is that the central characters see the true nature of the war more clearly than their fellow soldiers. Who, therefore, can condemn them? Certainly not those who have never experienced the fighting.

---

*A. D. Gristwood, *The Somme, Including Also The Coward* (London: Jonathan Cape, 1927). H. G. Wells, preface to *The Somme,* 9–12.

Gristwood's account of the war is deeply disenchanted, because he was unconvinced it was worth fighting, because his deep psychological and physical wounds blighted his life after he returned home, because his service as a private was an uncomfortable one for a cultivated man, and because with his ultrasensitive, "neurasthenic" nature he felt the fear, discomfort, and horror more acutely than most.

Throughout his book he is at pains to emphasize how low morale had sunk in the British army and how little there really was of the much-acclaimed comradeship or patriotism that allegedly kept troops cheerfully fighting. He gives the example of Forsyth, a soldier quite open in his repeated efforts to surrender. Gristwood acknowledges in his book that many men alongside him were trusting and dutiful, but in his view this was out of stupidity and a desire for self-protection. He accepts that some were brave—such as the four men from the battalion who carry Everitt in a stretcher at great hazard to the rear of the line—but more often, in his experience, he argues, soldiers in battle, himself included, regarded discretion as the better part of valor:

> Against what was evidently overwhelming fire, any advance might well be suicidal folly and in the absence of leadership or encouragement [*the platoon commander had been killed*], the law of self-preservation swept aside all discipline: since no one seemed to care what happened, men determined to play their own hands. No doubt that moment of hesitation marked the failure of the attack. Hitherto, while there had never been any pretence of enthusiasm, at least the attempt was being made. Now they were fatally quiescent. It is a commonplace of war that a man who takes cover during an advance will never get up again until the battle is over.*

Yet for all his persuasive detail, there is a lack of balance in his low estimate of human nature and in his own self-contempt. Because of this, his grim indictment of war lacks an essential element of tragedy. Better-known British authors like Frederic

*Ibid., 54–55.

Manning, Siegfried Sassoon, Richard Aldington, and V. M. Yeates have some of Gristwood's bitterness; their message is painful but mitigated by a relish for life and by human sympathy, which raises their work above his level. Nothing like the deep affection felt by these other writers for their comrades appears in his book. Nobody in it speaks in the tones of the stoical, grief-stricken Private Pritchard in Manning's *The Middle Parts of Fortune* when Corporal Tozer tries to comfort him after his friend has been killed during the Somme battle:

"That's all right, Corporal," answered Pritchard evenly. "Bein' sorry ain't going to do us'ns no manner o'good. We've all the sorrow we can bear of our own, wi'out troubling' ourselves wi' that o' other folk. We 'elp each other all we can, an' when we can't 'elp the other man no more, we must jest 'elp ourselves. But I tell thee, Corporal, if I thought life was never goin' to be no different, I'd as lief be bloody well dead myself."*

Although Donald Gristwood's service records have not survived, nor is there mention of him in battalion diaries, it has been possible to trace at least an outline of his pathetically short life. He was born in Catford, south of London, on 17 May 1893, the only son of James Arthur Gristwood, a commercial traveler for a City of London firm. Later, the Gristwood family moved to a more prestigious address in Purley, a Surrey village fast becoming absorbed into the metropolis. Gristwood attended local schools there, leaving at sixteen. Shortly afterward he joined the accounting department of the Liverpool and London Globe Insurance Company, a job he disliked increasingly. Five years passed. Then, in his words, "came 1914 and the pestilence."†

Until 1916 recruits for the rapidly expanding British army were all volunteers. Men joined up under intense social pressure as well as from genuine patriotic sentiments. Gristwood himself, who did not "take the King's shilling" until late in the summer of 1915, a year

---

*Frederic Manning, *The Middle Parts of Fortune, Somme and Ancre 1916* (1929; London: Peter Davies, 1977), 15.
†Gristwood, *The Somme*, 15.

into the war, did so without conviction, an uncomfortable position, as he put it in *The Somme:* "the doubter, the Agnostic, the sitter on the fence, is doubly damned in the hurly-burly. The enthusiasts on either side despise him, and he finds himself committed to an endless balancing of arguments."*

Although well educated and intelligent, he never became an officer, despite the heavy demand caused by casualties: in his 1933 will he was described as "formerly Rifleman 302064." From this service number and his correspondence, it seems likely that he enlisted originally in the third battalion of the London Rifle Brigade (LRB). The LRB was a territorial unit made up of men who in peacetime had worked in the financial heart of London as bankers, stockbrokers, salesmen, clerks, and office employees, and who had played at soldiering during weekends.

The third battalion was formed as a training unit to supply drafts for the first and second battalions as their numbers were depleted by casualties. By definition, therefore, it did not have the same esprit de corps. Nonetheless, despite a shortage of rifles and experienced instructors at the camps near London and on Salisbury Plain, where the men trained, the commanders had some success in overcoming this problem. A large draft of third-battalion men was sent to the first battalion around September 1916 to replace the massive losses during the Somme battle, which had begun in July. Gristwood was among those sent, and he took part in the very hard fighting at this time.

The first battalion had already been through the ordeal of the notorious first day of the Somme battle when the British army had lost around nineteen thousand killed and twice that number wounded, missing, or captured. In September the battalion's numbers were further severely reduced in two separate actions, but still, according to the London Rifles' official history, they maintained their morale. At the close of September, the first battalion, as part of General Sir Henry Rawlinson's Fourth Army, again advanced against the enemy. The high command were confident of success, after the capture of the German's third line of defenses. However, the

*Ibid., 146.

advance was slow and gave the Germans a chance to complete a fourth defensive line and begin a fifth and a sixth. Appalling weather conditions turned the chalk terrain, pulverized by shellfire, into a morass of sticky mud. Even so, General Haig, the British commander in chief, persisted in trying to break through. On 8 October, near Le Transloy, the first battalion suffered devastating losses, including sixteen of those in the same draft as Gristwood. Many more were killed and wounded in the subsequent rescue efforts throughout the night, much like the scenes Gristwood described. He himself was wounded in the leg, either then or earlier, and carried to a dressing station with shells raining down. "Great being carried shoulder high with testimonials whizzing all round,"* he told a comrade later. Thence he was taken to No. 5 Hospital at Rouen, and in the ship *Austurias* to the United Kingdom several months later—on what day it is not known, but it was not before the beginning of 1917—he was sent back to the Western Front, having been pronounced fit and this time joining the London Rifle Brigade's second battalion.

The Battle of the Somme petered out finally in early November, but by then the first battalion of the London Rifle Brigade was out of the fighting: of its 542 other ranks and 21 officers who had entered the fray on 1 October, 164 were dead or had died of wounds —some 30 percent of the attacking force. Only 108 men and 2 officers marched back to their rest billets by Trones Wood.

As for the second battalion of the London Rifles, to which, according to Gristwood's will, he was transferred at some time prior to 28 August 1917, the evidence is that for most of 1917 it was in good heart. Without newly unearthed documentation, there is no way of determining how much he was involved in the battalion's fighting from the time it arrived on the Continent in January 1917

---

*A. D. Gristwood to Moorat, letter, 27 October 1916, in private possession of K. W. Mitchinson, author of *Gentlemen and Officers: The Impact and Experience of War on a Territorial Regiment 1914–1918* (London: Imperial War Museum 1995) on the London Rifle Brigade. Thanks are owed to K. W. Mitchinson for his help on Gristwood's service career, which allows this introduction to put the record straight and furnishes important detail unavailable at the time I described it in *The Flower of Battle* (1996).

as part of the Fifty-eighth Division. From March, the second battalion was in and out of the line close to Arras where a major British offensive began early in April. In May the battalion captured with heavy losses the shattered village of Bullecourt in the German line. There was further intense fighting in this sector and others, with high casualties, throughout May and, with brief rests, into July.

In late August it went into reserve before being flung into the third battle of Ypres. On 20 September the Fifty-eighth Division, including Gristwood's battalion, launched an attack on enemy lines, known as the Battle of the Menin Road Ridge, which was destined to be the climax of the LRB second battalion's achievement as a unit. In the two days' fighting that followed, the Fifty-eighth Division took all its objectives and captured or killed a large number of German troops, but it paid a steep price in dead and wounded for this triumph. As a result of their success and courage, the second battalion's commanding officer was awarded the Distinguished Service Order Medal and another officer the Military Cross, while eighteen other ranks received the Military Medal and six the Distinguished Conduct Medal.

After a month's rest, the second battalion was back until mid-November in the hell of mud and shellfire for which the Passchendaele offensive will be forever remembered. By the end of October it was effectively little more than half its full establishment. Between mid-December and mid-January the battalion continued in the Flanders area, on working-party duty only. Then, on 29 January 1918, it was disbanded, possibly because it was no longer a viable fighting unit, and also because of the general reduction of battalions during this period. Its men were assigned to different London Territorial battalions.

How far does all this confirm Gristwood's disparaging account of the army in his two novels? As far as esprit de corps was concerned, the first battalion undoubtedly fought with great courage and tenacity during 1916. It also seems that Gristwood—at least during the same period—far from looking down on the other men, was genuinely concerned about their fate and that of his unit. This emerges from a letter he wrote on 27 October 1916 to Rifleman S. A. Moorat, followed by a Christmas card on 13 December while recovering from his wound in England. He observed darkly, "Fiendish rumours that 200 left of the Battn. and two officers, but personally didn't believe it." Elsewhere he referred with sympathy to comrades who had been wounded. His tone to his friend, though sardonic, had more than a trace of normality and camaraderie in it. He signed off with "Cheer O, Nearly 1917 (and if we can survive that, we can yet make a bid for three score years and ten) but of course, cui bono?"*

When he later came to write *The Somme,* either he deliberately discounted, for dramatic effect, the battalion companionship he had apparently felt in late 1916, or, more likely, his feelings of solidarity at that time had been eclipsed by the horrors he experienced the following year, when a profound despair set in, excluding memories of human warmth and selflessness.

Though esprit de corps seems also to have been strong in the second battalion during most of 1917, it is easy to see that despite initially having the characteristic spirited demeanor of the volunteer units, the soldiers of the second battalion had suffered such punishing casualties that by 1918 they would outwardly at least have seemed battle fatigued and despondent. Both first and second battalions enjoyed a reputation for steadiness, but there is evidence that the men in both units began to register unhappiness with the way they had been used in the big battles. Moreover, by February or March of that year, if Gristwood was still at the front, as his remarks in his book suggest, he would have found himself reassigned to yet another battalion, with few individuals in it that he recognized, a change known to have had a very demoralizing effect on those who experienced it. Battalion and divisional spirit can only be built up through prolonged training and companionship in action, and once units have been fragmented and their soldiers redistributed, months must pass before strong new identities emerge.

It is unsurprising, then, that Gristwood wrote with heavy irony of the infantry's outlook in early 1918, just before the German March Offensive, when the British army was driven into retreat: "It is a

*A. D. Gristwood to Moorat, letters, 27 October, 13 December 1916, K. W. Mitchinson (see note on p. xiii.).

damning admission, and one probably unique in the annals of war, but the spirit of the troops was not entirely excellent."* His father records him as having been wounded twice during his war service. Whether at that time Gristwood perpetrated the same self-mutilation that gets the protagonist of *The Coward* out of the fighting line, and whether this was his second wound, it is likely never to be learned; but if that story seems suspiciously like a personal confession, one must also remember that many soldiers felt conscience stricken after the war at having escaped their comrades' fate by a timely wound that took them home. Someone as depressed by shock and pain and as afflicted with nervous anxiety and self-loathing as Gristwood plainly became could easily have been capable of imagining himself guilty of cowardice, even if innocent of it.

Viewed historically, his judgment on the British infantry's morale at the time is too narrowly based to give a true overall picture. Far from collapsing in 1918, the army rallied, beat off other German assaults, and in late summer began to sweep the enemy back during the victorious "hundred days" of tough fighting, which by November had left the British Expeditionary Force as master of the field. Gristwood's purpose, however, was not to write military history but to hammer home the message that nobody should ever have been put through the hell of the Western Front, as he and his battle-strained comrades had been the previous two years.

After the war Gristwood returned to Purley still suffering from his wounds. By 1926 the monotony of his insurance company work and his ill health caused a nervous breakdown. On a rest cure in the Italian lakes, he resolved to leave the world of commerce. "I would do anything," he wrote bitterly, "that did not involve eating out of the public's hand with a view to persuading it to buy my employer's goods."† What he now sought was work in a library, a bookshop, or a publisher, but it was clear that he was most interested in becoming a writer. Fortunately, powerful help was at hand.

---

*Gristwood, *The Somme*, 133.
†A. D. Gristwood to H. G. Wells, letter, 4 November 1926, H. G. Wells Papers, University Library, University of Illinois, Urbana-Champaign.

As a boy in the 1870s, Gristwood's father had attended Mr. Morley's Academy in Bromley, southeast of London. One of his school companions there had been H. G. Wells, subsequently one of Britain's most important authors and prophets of the modern age. James Gristwood had only once seen his famous friend since then, but in 1926 he summoned up courage to write to him about his son's breakdown, his dreadful ordeal in the war, and his broken health. Could Wells, he wondered, help to find him a job in the world of books "he has read widely, & I think with discrimination and he has built up a library which does him credit."*

Wells was greatly moved. Like many other distinguished writers, he had elected to serve his country by writing war propaganda, but his conscience was uneasy knowing that not all he had written was the truth and unconvinced that either Britain's shrill wartime patriotism or her empire, which he despised, were objects for which it had been worth sacrificing nine hundred thousand lives or his own integrity. After the conflict, he sought to atone for this *trahison des clercs* by taking an antiwar stance. In Donald Gristwood he found a war victim to champion.

The younger Gristwood, overwhelmed by this interest in him, replied in his usual self-disparaging manner from his lakeside hotel: "I have spent an hour trying to put together something that did not seem affected, & yet would not too greatly offend your naturally critical eye."† He sent Wells what he had written on the scenery of the Somme battle: "I fear you are tortured by similar offerings daily, but if anything could stir a drowsy pen, it would be such a theme, & I should greatly appreciate your most ruthless criticism."‡ The correspondence with Wells from Gristwood's family that followed over the next seven years reveals much of the parents' anxious, perhaps overprotective, feelings about their son and something of Donald Gristwood's self-consciousness, shyness, and lack of social graces intensified by illness.

---

*Ibid., 29 September 1926.
†Ibid., 4 November 1926.
‡Ibid.

Within three months, with Wells's encouragement, *The Somme* was complete. Gristwood had by then decided to offer his book with another manuscript he had written some time before, that of *The Coward*, so that the two short novels could appear together in one volume. Wells was generous with advice, querying on grounds of taste, for instance, Gristwood's unkind observations about chaplains on the Western Front. These were characteristic of the book's general tone—and, indeed, padres tended to be popular objects of derision in war reminiscences, as in C. E. Montague's *Disenchantment* and Robert Graves's *Good-bye to All That*. Accounts of their absurdities may have been true in some soldiers' experience, but, as the real heroism of many clergy at the front shows, they were misleadingly one-sided.

In fact, Wells himself had not been one to spare parsons from criticism in his own books. Indeed, it is striking generally how much the note of ruthless contempt, the ominous atmosphere, and the egotistic, neurotic central characters in *The Somme* and *The Coward* resemble creations by Wells. Gristwood's protagonists are outsiders—in this resembling Griffin, in Wells's *Invisible Man*—clever, persecuted, despising the common herd. Wells had his reward for the support and inspiration he had given. His new novel, *Mr Blettsworthy on Rampole Island*, which came out in 1928, featured scenes from the World War, praised for their authenticity, in which he had paraphrased passages from Gristwood's book. Doubtless, Gristwood, grateful to his benefactor, accepted this as a compliment.

Gristwood insisted on keeping the chaplain paragraphs as a true record of what soldiers felt at the time. Only a few cuts were made in the end, and thanks to Wells's influence, the book was published by Jonathan Cape in October 1927. In his foreword Wells proclaimed it as essential evidence for any future history of the war of "the feelings and experiences of the directed undistinguished multitude, unwilling either to injure or be injured, caught in the machine."* He wisely made no claim (as critics were to make for *All Quiet on the Western Front* in 1929) that here at last was the Truth about the war.

*Wells, preface to Gristwood, *The Somme*, 9–12.

Wells's name ensured the book critical attention, and Captain Cyril Falls in his celebrated bibliography of war writing gave credit to Gristwood's skill, though he considered *The Coward* more likely to create militarists than pacifists in revolt against its "loathsome" leading character.* Edward Shanks, a fellow war veteran, dismissed in the *New Statesman* Gristwood's account as being, if true, "in no sense typical of the experiences of the ordinary private." He singled out for censure "a number of rather cheap and disagreeable sneers at officers and padres," as Wells had warned might happen. Shanks asserted confidently that "they are not likely to be read—and Mr Gristwood's propagandist journalese certainly does not deserve to be read—by future generations."†

However objectionable he found such comments, Gristwood was prepared to accept criticisms of his style, which as an aspiring author he was anxious to improve. But the writing, though sometimes labored, is in the main effective in conveying his desolate vision. The book, which sold around 2,100 copies, was reprinted in 1928. The following year, however, when public demand for antiwar books suddenly rocketed and sales of *The Somme* were likely to increase accordingly, Cape put it out of print. Gristwood's royalties came to no more than fifty pounds, the sum Wells had told him to expect.

Not long after, the elder Gristwood retired from the city. He and his family, including Donald, moved to Betchworth, a secluded Surrey village near the town of Dorking. There they lived in a mundane new house (still standing), ambitiously named "Avalon," in a modern development incongruous with its picturesque surroundings. Over the next few years Gristwood's efforts to find a publisher for future books failed, and his health deteriorated. He led a circumscribed invalid's existence, as he told Wells, "muddling about with doctors—hospitals, X-Rays, Nursing Homes and all the rest of the accursed paraphenalia [sic]."‡ He finally dropped all literary activity,

---

*Cyril Falls, *War Books: An Annotated Bibliography of Books about the Great War* (London: Greenhill Books, 1930), 276.
†New Statesman, 12 November 1927, 14
‡A. D.Gristwood to H. G.Wells, letter, I October 1932, Wells Papers, University of Illinois, Urbana-Champaign.

save some reviewing for the *Sunday Times* and the *World*. Dr. Brice Smith, the physician who looked after him over a long period, described him as "a highly nervous man,"[*] susceptible to violent nerve storms.

His parents were continually worried. In April 1933, Mrs. Gristwood sent for the doctor because, she said, her son was in a very disturbed state of mind. Gristwood confided to Brice Smith that he felt "desperate"[†] and replied with a nod of the head when the doctor asked him if he meant suicidal. An appointment with a London specialist was fixed for him on 24 April. That morning, his mother found him in a heavy sleep from which he could not be wakened. Despite strenuous efforts to revive him throughout that day and the next, he died. He was thirty-nine.

At the coroner's court, the jury returned a verdict of suicide. He had taken about one hundred grains of Veronal, a sleep-inducing drug—two and a half times more than the minimum fatal dose. The parents were too distressed to offer any reasons for the tragedy. This was left to the doctor, in whose view Gristwood's war wounds lay at its root: "his whole war experience knocked him off his mental balance."[‡] The story featured only in the local Dorking newspaper, which made no allusion to Gristwood having written a book or to his connection with a world-famous author. The elder Gristwood told Wells of their loss in a short note the day after it occurred, though saying nothing about what had caused his son's death.

James Gristwood died in 1941. In his will, drawn up just after the suicide, he left his wife and unmarried niece a life interest in his several properties, stipulating that when these were eventually sold, the money should go to various soldiers' charities. Gristwood's books—which must have included many of Donald's—were to be distributed to libraries, and to TOCH, the servicemen's religious organization set up during the Great War, the war which had ruined his only son's brief life.

---

[*]*Dorking and Leatherhead Advertiser,* 26 May 1933, 9
[†]Ibid.
[‡]Ibid.

Apart from his grave in Dorking cemetery, the book is A. D. Grist-wood's sole monument. Questioning even comradeship and courage as it did, it incensed some ex-servicemen proud of their record and failed to make the impact that the author hoped. It came too early to attract a wider readership. *The Somme* and *The Coward* are not masterpieces, but the author's readiness to abandon any pretense of gentlemanly reticence liberated him from many of the inhibiting literary conventions that often weaken war writing of that time. The power of *The Somme* lies in its unhappy voice. Gristwood spoke out where others dared not, for self-justification maybe, but also to tell the truth about the fighting as he understood it. "The rhetoric of a thousand journalists will never bring home to the civilian a tithe of what war is," he wrote. "The ghastly futility of the thing; its blasphemy of God and human nature; its contemptuous denial of Christianity; its mechanical cold-blooded cruelty—only those who saw these things face to face can measure their horror. And those who know cannot share their knowledge."*

Other Sources

Aldington, Richard. *Death of a Hero.* London: Chatto & Windus, 1929.

Cecil, Hugh. *The Flower of Battle.* South Royalton, Vt.: Steerforth Press, 1996.

Graves, Robert. *Good-bye to All That.* London: Jonathan Cape, 1929.

Life and Letters, 3 (November 1929).

Maurice, Frederick. Introduction to *The History of the London Rifle Brigade, 1859–1919.* London: Constable, 1921.

Montague, C. E. *Disenchantment.* London: Chatto & Windus, 1922.

New Statesman, 12 November 1927.

Sassoon, Siegfried. *The Memoirs of an Infantry Officer.* London: Faber & Faber, 1930.

Second London Rifles. Battalion Diary. National Archives, Kew, UK, WO 95/3005.

Wells, H. G. Letters from Gristwood family, 1926–36. University Library, University of Illinois, Champaign-Urbana.

————. *Mr Blettsworthy on Rampole Island.* London: Ernest Benn, 1928.

Yeates, V. M. *Winged Victory.* London: Jonathan Cape, 1934.

---

*Gristwood, *The Somme,* 146–47

PREFACE TO THE FIRST EDITION

THE Story of the Great War is being written from a thousand points of view. It has produced, and continues to produce, a crop of wonderfully vivid and illuminating books as unprecedented as itself. A vast quantity of weed and rubbish mingles with this literature; some of it may be for a time overgrown and unrecognized. No phase in history has ever been so copiously and penetratingly recorded. A time will come when all this vast accumulation of matter will need to be revised and condensed for the use of the ordinary reader in a new age.

No one book will stand out as the whole complete story. That would be impossible of a system of events so enormous, various and many-sided. It will be necessary to group authorities and witnesses to convey any conception of so complex a catastrophe. But I imagine that in the future, when copyrights have expired and the intelligent popular publisher gets to work for his more intelligent and abundant public, there will be for the Great War, and possibly for one or two other phases of this history we are living now, collections of books and stories, little encyclopædias of presentation, planned to give altogether something like a living many-sided view of the immense multiplex occurrence. Such groupings of books is inevitable in the days to come. It is quite possible that for a backbone, from a Whitehall point of view, the English reading student of the future will follow the vigorous informed history Mr. Winston Churchill is unfolding. There he will have, admirably done, the geographical framework, the dates and the traditional heroic picture of the national struggle. Supplementing that he will have histories by other leading figures of this or that campaign in which they played their part. Lawrence's *Seven Pillars* (*Revolt in the Desert*), vivid, intense, will, for example, be an inevitable associate. But it is not for me to attempt any list of 'best books' in this field. Whatever assemblage of leaders' versions we read, the history will still have something largely hollow about it until we bring in the other less eloquent side of the affair, the feelings and experiences of the directed undistinguished multitude, unwilling either to injure or be injured, caught in the machine.

That multitude has found a voice in this war, as it has never found a voice in any preceding convulsion. It is extraordinarily important for the welfare of the world that our sons and successors should hear that testimony also. Something of the quality of the common men in the war has been preserved to us in a collection of war letters from the ranks made by Mr. James Milne, and in such a book as Enid Bagnold's *Diary Without Dates* and a number of other kindred works we get the sympathetic record of other experiences of the obscure. But the million British dead have left no books behind. What they felt as they died hour by hour in the mud, or were choked horribly with gas, or relinquished their reluctant lives on the stretchers, no witness tells. But here is a book that almost tells it, and that is why I am writing to claim a place for Mr. Gristwood's unheroic tale of *The Somme* side by side with the high enthusiastic survey of Mr. Winston Churchill. A. D. Gristwood has some very notable qualities; he writes clearly and unaffectedly and he remembers with a courageous clearness. Most of us have the trick of strangling and making away with all our more disagreeable memories; instinctively we destroy the record of how miserable we were or how afraid we were. Mr. Gristwood has had the relentless simplicity to recall things as they were; he was as nearly dead as he could be without dying, and he has smelt the stench of his own corruption. This is the story of millions of men – of millions. This is war as the man in the street will get it if it comes again. The stories the generals and statesmen tell are the stories of a small minority. If our sons read these alone they may fall under the delusion that war is a bright eventful going to and fro in London, slightly dangerous but not uncomfortable visits to the front, an occasional stimulating air-raid, vivid news of victory or defeat, which only makes us brace ourselves up more bravely – to keep the 'Tommies' at it. Some of us got it that way. I did for one – as it happened. But the common man's share, our sons must understand, lacked all that bright and cheerful latitude. He felt caught, he felt driven, he was tormented, he saw his fate approach him, and in the end he was mutilated or died very wretchedly. The chances for most of those who dream of the stern resistances and triumphant advances of Armageddon, if another war occurs, are a thousand to one that it is Mr. Gristwood's path they will be invited to follow and not Mr. Winston Churchill's. This book is a very important book therefore, in spite of its author's modest manner. It is a living page in the true history of democracy. It is a book that every boy with a taste for soldiering should be asked to read and ponder. And it is a profoundly interesting and moving book.

H. G. WELLS

THE SOMME

'War is the medicine of God.'

TREITSCHKE

INTRODUCTION

BEFORE the world grew mad, the Somme was a placid stream of Picardy, flowing gently through a broad and winding valley northwards to the English Channel. It watered a country of simple rural beauty: for long miles the stream fed lush water-meadows, where willows and alders and rushes slumbered in the sun, and cornlands and fat orchards supported a race of canny peasants. Cosy, sleepy-seeming hamlets lay scattered over the land, and among these ancient towns and villages only Amiens styled herself a City, and admitted the noisy strife of commerce. For the rest, far from the fever of life, the banks of the stream yielded lairs for patient fishermen: punts followed the tortuous channels of the river; tall rows of sentinel poplars guarded the highways of the Republic; wide dry downlands swelled between the rivers; life seemed a matter of sowing and reaping, of harvest-home and neighbourly chat over wine and syrop in the Café Delphine.

And then came 1914 and the pestilence.

I

I⊤ was a gloriously hot and sunny day in September. The Loamshires were in newly won trenches outside Combles. The town, or the battered husk that represented it, had fallen that morning, but the battalion was far from feeling any flush of victory. Even the unheard-of event of the French advancing past Combles in clearly visible columns of fours failed to rouse them. Every one was languid and weary and dispirited.

The trenches had been abandoned by the Germans only yesterday, and everywhere lay scattered their arms and clothing. And not only arms! Sprawling over the parapets were things in rags of grey and khaki that had once been men. As far as the clothing went nothing extraordinary was visible, but the dead men's faces were black with a multitude of flies. These indeed were the worst horror. Everywhere they found carrion and ordure, and, disturbed by the traffic of the trench, the buzzing cloud revealed raw festering flesh where once had been a happy human countenance. Fresh from such a feast, they settled on living men and shared their rations: sluggish, bloated creatures, blue and green and iridescent. Well was Beelzebub named the Prince of Flies!

Sometimes the Germans had buried their dead in the floor of the trench, where, baking in the sun, the earth had cracked into star-shaped fissures. A foot treading unwarily here sunk suddenly downwards,

disturbing hundreds of white and wriggling mag-
gots. In one place a hand with blue and swollen
fingers projected helplessly from the ground. 'O
death, where is thy sting? O grave, where is thy
victory?'

An order had been given that, in consolidating the
trench, as soon as pick or shovel should disturb the
dead, the hole should be filled in again and the earth
beaten down. Often fragments of blanket or clothing gave warning, and sometimes the sudden gush of
escaping gases. Not a hundred yards to the left lay
Leuze Wood, captured by the battalion a fortnight
ago. Little progress had been made since then, and,
in so exposed a position, the dead could not always be
buried. Moreover, fatigue and the indifference of
desperation made their presence of little account, and
thus there lay in the billows of tumbled earth a company of dead men half-buried, flung there like pup-
pets thrown down by a child. Close to the trench a
man of the Loamshires stood nearly upright, buried
to the waist, his arms fast bound to his side, his
glassy eyes wide open to the sky, his face stained livid
yellow from the fumes of an explosion. Who he was
no one knew: doubtless his dear ones were writing to
him in hope and trust for his welfare: doubtless they
had prayed that night for his safety. And all the time
he stood there, glaring upwards as though mutely
appealing from Earth to Heaven.

The carrion reek of putrefaction filled the wind.
For twenty-four hours drum-fire had deafened all the

world, and sleep had been a matter of dozes between hours of horror. Hostile shelling, occasional casualties, the dead weight of fatigue, the grim barrenness of what was called a 'victory,' the vista of months ahead – fear ever lying in wait to grow to panic – small wonder if these things had damped men's spirits! There had indeed been current that morning rumours of relief, promptly discountenanced by experienced cynics. (And every one who had been in France for a month was a cynic.) There were even tales of a Divisional Rest for a month, laughed to scorn even more readily.

Hence the glittering wonder of the event. To a party of men carrying petrol-tins on a water-fatigue appeared an immaculate being in red tabs. He seemed strangely out of place in that Golgotha – and yet not so out of place. 'Who are you men?' 'Tenth Loamshires, sir.' 'What are you doing?' 'Water party, sir.' 'You don't want any water. You're relieved to-night. Go down to the "Cookers" and wait orders there. Don't take those things back – the less movement we have the better.' Thus the beneficent decree of the Dynast. Soulless plodding changed to eager haste; tongues were unloosed. A sergeant was heard to say: 'That ends the bloody Somme for us,' and in less than a minute every one was repeating the words like a hope of salvation.

The 'Cookers' lay in a deep hollow a mile to the rear of the line. The place was known as 'Death Valley,' by no means without reason. There were the foremost batteries, and the fatigue party waited until dusk in a whirlpool of hurry. The 'Big Push,' to use the euphemistic cant of the day, was in full cry. Always new guns were arriving, and ammunition-limbers, ration-wagons, water-carts, field-kitchens, mules, stores of the Royal Engineers, camouflage materials, corrugated iron, timber, barbed wire, sandbags in thousands. No lorries or ambulances could reach Death Valley, however, which lay far from paved roads among the uplands of the Somme. The hill-side tracks had been utterly obliterated by the weeks of shell-fire since the blood-stained 1st July, and all the countryside was a wilderness. To write 'a wilderness' is easy, but to realize the appearance of the landscape you must have seen it. Thereabouts the country is open downland, after the manner of Sussex, largely grass-covered, and sprinkled capriciously with rare patches of woodland. From the crests of the ridges mile upon mile of country was visible, and everywhere the land lay utterly waste and desolate. Not a green thing survived the harrowing of the shells. Constant barrages had churned the land into a vast desert of shell-craters, one intersecting another like the foul pock-markings of disease. To look over these miles of blasted country, thus scarified to utter nakedness, was to see a lunar landscape, lifeless, arid and accursed.

At night this sense of other-worldliness was stronger than ever. In the dense darkness, where

to show a light was probably suicide, the dismal
sea of craters was lit only by the flash of guns and
the noiseless ghastly glare of Verey lights. In the
white radiance of the magnesium flares all things
seemed to await judgment, and the ensuing utter
darkness came with the suddenness of doom.
From dusk to dawn they traced in the sky their
graceful parabolas, hanging long in the air as
though unwilling to cease their brooding over
it. Always they seemed cold, revealing, pitiless,
illuminating with passionless completeness this
foul chaos of man's making, unutterably sad and
desolate beneath the stars. From far behind the
line you could trace the course of the trenches by
their waxing and waning, and the veriest child at
home knew the danger of their all-revealing splen-
dour.

By day the hills were deserted, and only in the
valleys and hollows was movement visible. In daylight those open ridges might only be crossed in
safety by small parties of perhaps twenty men – lost
in the vastness of the landscape. Larger parties
drew gun-fire, and road traffic could by no means
face the wilderness. It was in such small parties
that the Loamshires had first found their way to
Combles from the flesh-pots of Amiens: their first
sight of the Somme battlefield was gained from the
Crucifix above Death Valley. This ancient iron
cross, rusty, bent, and ominous, yet remained as a
notorious landmark on the hill-side, and from the

shattered trenches near by they looked forward
across the valley to a hideous welter of dust and
smoke and intolerable noise. A heavy bombardment was in progress, and great spouts of flying
earth sprang skywards unceasingly. Not a yard of
the tortured earth appeared immune from these
volcanoes, and it seemed impossible that a man
could live five minutes within the zone of their
tumult. And yet they knew that men were facing
their utmost shock and horror not a mile from where
they were standing, and it was all too obvious that
their turn awaited them Tiny dust-coloured figures
could be seen moving amid the welter, surviving
by a miracle. The continuous hullabaloo of guns
smote their ears with a vicious perseverance of
shock. There, across the valley, lay the reeking
core of this desolation, smoking, flaming, forcing
itself with hideous toil and confusion towards an
unknown decision. For miles to north and south
stretched this artificial Hell, and the reek of it
darkened the autumn sky.

Within the region of desolation the rare woods
were matchwood only, shattered stumps of trees,
bristles of timber splintered and torn to fantastic
shreds and patches. Each wood was a maze of
ruined trenches, obstructed by the fallen riven
trunks of trees, dotted with half-obliterated dug-
outs, littered with torn fragments of barbed wire.
This, indeed, was largely twisted and broken by
shell-fire, but in rusted malignancy it yet remained

22

fiercely hindering. Immediately after their final capture (for commonly they changed hands half a dozen times in a week) these woodlands of the Somme represented the apotheosis of Mars. There lay the miscellaneous débris of war – men living, dying and dead, friend and foe broken and shattered beyond imagination, rifles, clothing, cartridges, fragments of men, photographs of Amy and Gretchen, letters, rations, and the last parcel from home. Shells hurling more trees upon the general ruin, the dazing concussion of their explosion, the sickly sweet smell of 'gas,' the acrid fumes of 'H.E.,' hot sunshine mingling with spouts of flying earth and smoke, the grim portent of bodies buried a week ago and now suffering untimely resurrection, the chatter of machine-guns, and the shouts and groans of men – such were the woods of the Somme, where once primroses bloomed and wild rabbits scampered through the bushes.

Rarely are there many men visible, and the few are hot, grimy and exhausted beneath their ludicrous shrapnel helmets shaped like pie-dishes. They move slowly because they can by no means move otherwise. The mud from recent rains has caked on the skirts of their great-coats, and their boots and puttees are coated white and yellow with soil. Probably they last shaved a week ago, and have since washed in shell-holes. They are irritable, quarrelsome, restless even in their fatigue, with dark shadows beneath their eyes and drawn, set faces. That little group carrying a stretcher, plodding slowly, with eyes fixed on the ground and faces of a strange dead, yellowish hue, is leaving the front line. For perhaps forty-eight hours the men have been lying in holes and ditches, 'being shelled to hell.' They passed the time as best they might – smoking, dozing, eating, quarrelling, drinking, cleaning rifles that were instantly fouled again by the drifting dust. They dared not leave their holes even to relieve the demands of nature. Vermin maddened them and only ceased their ravages in the cool of the night. Occasionally a shell struck home and they saw their friends mangled to red tatters. Sometimes men were numbed to idiocy by concussion; sometimes they were buried alive in the earthquake of a collapsing trench; sometimes a lucky man secured an arm wound and 'packed up' for hospital before their envying eyes. Perhaps an exposed position involved digging. Chalk is tough to handle, and the spur of shell-fire, if it goads to exertion, does little to invigorate. And this is why they seem dazed, with the haggard beaten air of suffering children. But at least their faces are set towards the old familiar world of trees and fields and farm-yards; of women and children; of red-roofed estaminets where vin rouge restores the hearts of men, of straw barns where lives oblivion.

It will be said that here is no trace of the 'jovial Tommy' of legend, gay, careless, facetious, facing

24

all his troubles with a grin and daunting the enemy by his light-heartedness. We all know the typical Tommy of the War Correspondents – those ineffable exponents of cheap optimism and bad jokes. ''Alf a mo', Kaiser,' is the type in a nutshell. A favourite gambit is the tale of the wounded man who was smoking a Woodbine. Invariably he professes regret at 'missing the fun,' and seeks to convey the impression that bayonet fighting is much like a football match, and even more gloriously exciting. It was such trash that drugged men's minds to the reality of war. Every one actively concerned in it hated it, and the actual business of fighting can never be made anything but devilish. It is even divested of the old hypocritical glories of music and gay colours (and so far, indeed, the change is for the better). The patriots at home urged that 'it was necessary to keep up the nation's spirit; nothing would have been gained by unnecessary gloom,' but a people that must be doped to perseverance with lies is in an evil case, and the event of these Bairnsfather romances was a gigantic scheme of falsehood. How bitterly it was resented the nation never knew.

From Death Valley the Loamshires marched over the hills to Meaulte. At the tail-end of the march they were dog-weary, but twelve hours' sleep on straw went far to restore them. For twenty-four hours the joy of release was undimmed. With clean, vermin-free underclothing, and after a long night's rest and a hot shower-bath, once more it was possible to think sanely; the lowering cloud of urgent danger was lifted for a season. Perhaps it was a cynical enjoyment, but the bands that played in the square, the cosy, crazy little shops where wrinkled old women sold delicious coffee, the roaring tide of khaki, drunk and sober, in the streets, made them forget altogether those thousands suffering and dying in the furnace not half a dozen miles away. Meaulte lies on the edge of the 'old front line' and, to normal eyes, was hideous enough. The houses had been shelled to greater or less dilapidation, and dust lay thick on every road and yard. The shops, even when intact, were blighted with a hopeless dirt and squalor. Hardly a house remained in occupation, and the few inhabitants, lost in the crowd of troops, sold coffee, vin rouge, biscuits, chocolate, tinned fruits and cigarettes as the last resource against ruin. Every garden had run wild, and the autumn flowers were dusty and stunted among the weeds. It was a foul-mouthed, jostling throng that filled the streets, their pockets temporarily full and hearts light by reason of a week's respite. Small wonder drunkenness and debauchery ran riot in the place. They were the only means of forgetting.

From this grey pandemonium the men of the Loamshires hoped to march westwards again to the real France beyond the battle zone. 'Divisional Rest' was due, and already that month the brigade had lost more than half its strength at Leuze Wood.

New drafts had restored their numbers, but some weeks of work together would be required to restore the battalions to efficiency. But, quenching the sergeant's pious hope, came on the second morning the order to 'parade for pay and stand by ready to move off in an hour's time.' The news came like a blow, and the delayed pay an hour before departure seemed a refinement of exasperation. Of what use was money if the creditors were to be moved away from all chance of spending it? During pay-parade the company commanders, haranguing their men, told them that they were to return to the 'forward area' (blessed euphemism) for ten days, and that the battalion's sole duty lay in the construction of a forward-trench as close as might be to the German lines. They were assured, with a particularity that seemed almost suspicious, that during this 'tour in the line' they were to be used only as pioneers. Certainly they had done Yeomen's service on the Somme, both on the 1st July at Gommecourt and on the 9th September at Leuze Wood, and undoubtedly the new drafts were inexperienced and unassimilated. But already the rumoured Divisional Rest had been cut down from a month to a day, and dark suspicions grew like the rank weeds of Meaulte.

Trones Wood of ill memory was their destination, and the march there filled the greater part of two days. After a night in old German dugouts, the official Reserve position were found to

be nothing more than a series of shelter trenches
midway between Trones Wood and Guillemont.
These were the merest slots in the ground, none
more than five feet deep. Wrapping themselves in
blankets and ground-sheets, and covering the tops
of the trenches with pilfered timber and sheets of
corrugated iron, they made themselves as comfort-
able as might be. These narrow ditches resembled
the drainage-trenches of a London suburb in the
heyday of its development towards villadom, but
the grimly humorous found a resemblance to
graves. By good management it was just possible
to curl up head to head in the slots, and the impedi-
menta of equipment were jammed haphazard into
holes and corners. After dark no lights were allowed
above ground, but, by shutting in a section of
trench with ground-sheets, the feeble illumination
of candles was available to those who had the good
fortune to possess any. Crawling along these narrow
alley-ways at night, dodging beneath ingenious
erections of blankets, stumbling over a long litter
of men and equipment, you would imagine yourself
in an overcrowded coal-mine, where fools performed
the simplest tasks with incredible toil. To turn,
you must stand up, and to venture out of the
trench was to invite the immediate disaster of falling headlong into a shell-hole. Once you had lost
your bivouac it might take you half an hour to
recover it.

Fortunately, the rain held off until the evening of

the Loamshires' departure. Even two hours had sufficed to transform the trenches into slimy morasses, with equipment and personal belongings fast sinking into the mud. Utterly forlorn these 'homes' seemed in their inundation, and, with nowhere to sit in comfort, men were the less sorry to leave them. Two days and nights saw them back again, so exhausted after their march that it was easy enough to fall asleep in the rain, often with nothing but a wet ground-sheet between the sleeper and a puddle. This time they occupied other trenches behind the wood, wider and less exasperatingly crowded. Here it was necessary to carve shelters in the sides of the trenches, using rubber sheets and blankets as the outer trenchward wall. Coiled up in these lairs, you could at least avoid the rain, and by sharing your bivouac it was even possible to lie warm. (To neutralize this luxury, the lice were the more active in snugger quarters.)

For several days their time was passed chiefly in salvage-fatigues. These involved the tiresome quartering of long acres of ground, and the collection and sorting into a variegated dump of all the litter of the battlefield. Not far from Trones Wood a blown-in trench held thousands of Mills bombs. These ingenious weapons are rendered harmless by a steel safety-pin, which rusts with damp. So long as they are undisturbed they are innocuous, but they have been known to lie forgotten and unheeded for weeks only to explode with fatal

29

results at an inadvertent kick. Thus it was delicate work disinterring them from the earth and débris in which they were nearly buried; but by a fluke of good fortune none had rusted sufficiently to fracture the pins, and there were no casualties.

In fine weather they were almost happy, and, dog-tired always, sound sleep came as a gift in the most cramped quarters. In the freshness of the morning the breakfasts of fragrant bacon were glorious indeed. The hot strong tea, and white bread far better than they were getting at home, were wolfed with eager appetite, and always there was a rush to the sooty dixie for the sake of the bacon-fat and greasy crackling that afford so tasty a dish when bread is used to sop them. Often porridge was added, so thick that it was possible to invert the dixie and no harm done. Unaffectedly living to eat, meals and mails were the only landmarks in monotonous days. For dinner came potatoes boiled in their skins and nondescript watery stew. On gala days roast beef appeared, and sometimes duff took the place of nauseous rice.

Apart from fatigues, drill consisted only in the inspection of rifles, but excuse for a full-dress parade was found in a message from the Brigadier. To hear his sacred words the battalion was drawn up in mass behind the wood, where a prying aeroplane might have stirred the enemy's artillery to serious activity. (But obviously risks must be run to hear a General's voice.) It seemed that that great man loved his men like a father, and that his children were to be praised for their prowess. They had done splendidly, and the high standard attained was never to be lowered. To the old hands the General expressed his thanks; to the new he said approximately 'Go thou and do likewise.' All and sundry were bidden 'never to forget the traditions of their battalion and brigade,' and it was obvious that storms were to be expected. The proceedings terminated with the distribution of 'Divisional Cards,' for all the world like prizes at a Sunday-school Treat, and the shame of the recipients was only equalled by the ribaldry of the audience. For these cards certified that the holder had distinguished himself in action at such a time and such a place, and even bore the signature of Olympus. The theory was that by this means a spirit of emulation was aroused, and it was reckoned that three of these cards meant a military medal in the rations. 'The Tommies are such children!' Such was life in Reserve.

II

A WEEK later the Loamshires were still behind Trones Wood. There were rumours that the Fusilier Battalion of the Brigade had 'done a stunt' that day, and during the afternoon a barrage on the left flank confirmed the story. These same rumours declared that in the event of 'the stunt being a wash-out' (in other words, some hundreds of men being killed to no purpose), the Loamshires were certain to 'have a cut at it.' To most of the men of the new drafts this was the final calamity. Six weeks in a quiet part of the Belgian line had given them little realization of the wholesale slaughter of a big offensive. War in the north was static, a leisurely thing to be studied and assimilated, an orderly business concern calculated to last for centuries. There on the Somme the pace was so hot that all men realized it could not outlast the autumn. If a decision could be reached before the rains, well; otherwise a third war-winter as a prelude to the easy optimism of yet another 'spring push!' Revolving these pleasant themes, and feeding on peculiarly lurid scraps of reminiscence with which, as novices, they had been favoured by the veterans, it would have seemed there was ample excuse for a sleepless night. As a matter of unromantic fact, neither the forebodings of to-morrow's transactions nor the howitzer battery not fifty yards away prevailed in the least against the drug of the past month's labours.

Midnight awoke them. To the weary men curled up in their blankets came the order, abrupt and stentorian: 'Get ready to move off. Hurry — there's no time to waste.' (As though the whole business were anything but a grotesque waste of time.) In the dense darkness patches of light showed candles in sheltered corners. From the murmur of talk only oaths could be distinguished, for every one knew the meaning of an unexpected midnight call. The battalion was 'for it' — time would show to what extent. In an instant the old man of the sea was firmly in his saddle again, the familiar incubus of vague anxiety and lurking dread. It was owing to his temporary dethronement that bedtime and forgetfulness were the boons of the day.

It was a mad scramble to collect the paraphernalia of equipment — a day's rations had of course been distributed overnight — but somehow the various straps and buckles were adjusted over greatcoats, and the rifles, gas-masks and ground-sheets slung and stowed as well as might be. In half an hour the battalion was strung along the road in column of fours, desperately tired, vaguely apprehensive, yawning with sleepiness, and with a temper blown to rags. Roll was called and flurried stragglers literally unearthed from their strayed paths. What was the game? Where were they going? No one knew, but the line was their obvious destination.

Progress was maddeningly slow. In the darkness the road was blocked with all manner of traffic —

c

lorries, ambulances, limbers, troops coming and going, fatigue-parties bearing strange burdens. So dense was the gloom that one rank could hardly see another, and every halt meant a stumbling collision and a hearty interchange of curses. Soon it was necessary to leave the road, and the column divided into two single files on the banks by the wayside. There the shelled ground provided a succession of pitfalls and invisible holes opened beneath vainly groping feet. Rifles make good sounding-rods, but always men were stumbling and falling, collapsing with a crash of rifle and equipment, often sousing themselves liberally with mud and water in the deeper craters. The language was epic, and to the blind audience the humour of these invisible catastrophes far outweighed their exasperation to the victim. But before the spectators had done laughing they themselves were impartially engulfed.

At one point in the road a horse-ambulance had tilted sideways into a huge shell-hole in the pavé, and, always in utter darkness, a mob of men was trying to right it. The helpless wounded on the stretchers had some of them been canted into the mud of the road, and others were clinging desperately to the straps of their cots. The groans in the darkness, the confusion of the traffic blocked round the ambulance, the babble of men and mules jostling in the mud, made a fantastic extremity of misery.

At the end of the first mile the companies sepa-

rated to artillery-formation, and the connecting
files had the best of the bargain: at least they were
able to walk without continual collisions. For an
interminable time the sorry procession stumbled
slowly forward. It would advance perhaps a hundred yards, halt for five minutes, advance fifty yards,
and halt again, ever without apparent rhyme or
reason. Vindictive messages were passed from the
rear! 'Why the devil don't we move on?' No one
knew, and no answer ever returned from the van.
After each halt the pace was rushed to the next,
where the ranks concertinaed in abrupt collision.
At such times the messages grew frantic. ' "B"
Company lost touch in rear.' 'Halt in front.' 'Step
short.' 'Why don't they run all the way?' And then
a long interval of querulous questioning: 'Are they
all up in rear?' 'Where the hell is "A" Company?'
until the legion of the lost ones closed up, sweating
and blasphemous. The rear of the column invariably suffers on these occasions, and it is incredibly
easy to lose connection in the dark over rough
ground.

Ten minutes' rest followed two hours' march-
ing (to all, that is, save those unfortunates who
were still frantically 'closing up'). Collapsing on a
muddy bank, half the men fell instantly asleep, careless where they were lying and anxious only to be
let alone. Roused after all too short a halt, the
battalion now left the roads for what had once
been fields, but were now a greasy wilderness of

holes and ridges. To avoid straying, the battalion formed one long file, and each man strained eyes and muscles to keep in touch with his leader: it was a mystery how the guide found his way through the darkness. A little ahead shells were falling, and soon the whole line was under fire. This was no heavy bombardment, however – merely the desultory shelling of lines of communication. All routes were picked out by the hawk-eyed aeroplanes, and every road and track scientifically 'searched' nightly with high-explosive. The 'four-point fives' whistled and moaned through the darkness, growing to a nerve-shaking, vicious hiss when near enough to be judged 'nasty.' The orange flash of their explosion glared ahead and behind and on either side, and often it seemed that shells had fallen right among the men. But they could pitch astonishingly near without physical damage, and there were few casualties. It is the moral effect of their shattering explosion, the dread of the rising whine of their approach, that gives them half their value.

Out in the fields the mud was thicker, and the task of putting one foot before the other absorbed every ounce of energy. The bog sucked greedily at heel and toe and only released embedded feet reluctantly. A fall into the morass plastered men from head to foot, and rifles became clotted and utterly useless. Occasionally it was necessary to cross a trench, and few cared to risk a leap in the dark.

More usually a man clambered down the slippery bank, falling into mud and water at the bottom. The rifle of the man ahead served as a grapnel to drag him up again, and he in his turn helped his neighbour. At first the Verey lights only just climbed above the curve of the ridges ahead, but soon they rose higher and yielded welcome light. Also they revealed twisted bodies beside the track, husks of men whose warfare was accomplished. It was peculiarly horrible to fall face downwards on a dead man. The rattle of snipers and machine-guns grew louder, but in the morass of mud in front of the field-guns raiding was impossible and the firing was scanty. From one trouble they were free: all the barbed wire had been blown to tatters by the shelling of weeks.

Dawn broke about four o'clock and the battalion was still far from its destination. A daylight relief was evidently to be attempted, for by this time it was known that the Fusiliers had been badly cut up, and that they were utterly incapable of holding the line. In the absence of communication trenches dawn was the more dangerous, but at least it was possible to see foothold, and the helpless blundering in the darkness yielded to more purposeful labours. Also, the friendly daylight put an end to the staggering concussion of unsuspected guns a yard or so away, and some kind of world, dismal and shattered indeed, but welcome after the chaos of the night, gradually took shape from the darkness.

37

Some complicated manœuvres of company formation followed in the grey dawning, and this involved an apparently aimless circling round a group of splintered trees. After an hour no advance had been made, and it was broad daylight when, in parties of ten and twenty, the Loamshires straggled over the last ridge. Thus clearly visible, there seemed no reason why they should not be annihilated; but the enemy preferred to encourage them, and the shelling grew no harder. The front line was sited on the forward slope of a line of low hills, and the Fusiliers were leaving it as the Loamshires arrived. No need for them to report that they had had a bad time! Their dead littered the ground and every whole man was helping a wounded comrade. They grinned through pallid faces at their successors and vanished slowly behind the ridge.

It was an unutterable relief to reach journey's end, however dangerous. After seven hours' arduous struggle, the last ounce of energy seemed drained from them. Sweat had made every one thirsty; they thought of nothing but drink and sleep. 'The line,' they found, was nothing but a winding muddy ditch, never deep enough to shelter a man standing upright, wasting beneath the assaults of the rain, and utterly useless against accurate shelling. Crowding in eagerly enough, however, the new-comers crouched monkey-wise in the trench and lit battered cigarettes.

On that forward slope of the hill the view ahead covered several miles. Across the shallow valley they saw a dense line of trees, little shattered by shell-fire and in startling contrast to the desolation behind them. The pile of rubble that represented Les Bœufs lay immediately to their rear behind the crest of the ridge. Not far ahead patches of green appeared among the tumbled heaps of brown earth, and far away on the left was a church spire. This was Bapaume, the goal of all their hopes and the key to victory. With Bapaume fell Cambrai and Berlin itself, said the pundits, and fools believed them. They were thus on the edge of the wilderness, and there, apparently within reach, was a green world of grass and trees and villages. One desperate plunge forward and the quagmire would be left behind! But alas! not a step forward was possible without the guardian barrage, churning those green fields to a morass, smashing villages to mouldering ruins, obliterating the fair face of Nature. Thus the Allies dragged behind them an ever-lengthening trail of ruin, while the Germans retired ever to clean lands and uninterrupted roads. White cotton clusters of bursting shrapnel showed the position of the enemy's lines at the bottom of the valley; otherwise they were invisible, with never a sign of wire. It seemed an easy thing to walk down that gentle slope towards the trees, but there was abundant evidence that others had tried and failed.

By this time rain was falling heavily, and the trench was slimy, cold and sodden. Thanks

to somebody's blunder, the men found themselves
so crowded in their muddy ditch that they stood
shoulder to shoulder, unable even to move. An
unlucky shell in such circumstances is ruinous, and
desperate messages were passed to the flanks.
Stragglers in vain besought shelter, and, the shelling
growing heavier, took cover in some blown-in dug-
outs immediately to the rear. These naturally opened
towards the enemy, but yet afforded in their farthest
recess a meagre shelter.

After a deal of shuffling and shifting, the men in
the trench found elbow-room and settled down to
the task of enlarging the 'funk-holes.' These were
the merest niches cut beneath the parapet, and
afforded at best but an uncomfortable seat. Their
strength lay in their moral value, which consisted
in bringing the heads of tenants well below the
skyline. They were utterly inadequate for protection against shells of the meanest calibre, but it is
well known that even a blanket gives a grotesquely
deceptive confidence. The blanket merely shuts out
the sight of the barrage, but its solace is undoubted,
and the ostrich justified. The line of the bombardment seemed to be towards the village some twenty
yards behind the trench, and the shelling was undoubtedly growing heavier. A few shells even
pitched short before the parapet and news arrived
of several casualties. The trench had no traverses
and the obtuse angles in the curves of it did little
to localize the effect of direct hits. The whizz-

bangs seemed to skim the parapets, and it was difficult to believe that a man could stand upright and save his head. At all events no one was disposed to try the experiment. Their sole comfort was that the softness of the ground provided frequent 'duds.'

Tom Everitt's platoon in 'C' Company occupied a section of the ditch near the opening of a shallow communication trench running forward down the hill. The smashed entrance of a dug-out sheltered the platoon commander and his batman, revealed intermittently behind a flapping fragment of blanket. The officer, Higgins by name, confined himself to alternate draughts of brandy and blasphemy: the men outside could avail themselves only of the latter. Contrary to the accepted theory, they by no means 'worshipped him,' and their dealings with him were confined strictly to business transactions. As an officer, Higgins was a privileged person evading, by virtue of his office, all the hard work and much of the discomfort. The danger, they admitted, he shared: certainly a man with the confidence and aplomb requisite to maintain a commission was a fool to do anything but accept one.

In the absence of brandy, Everitt redressed the balance by lurid grousing. How sick of it all he was, mere words could never tell, but recurring bouts of querulousness showed his nerves in rags. Why the devil couldn't Jim keep his infernal rifle to himself? That was the third time his laboriously erected rainproof shelter had collapsed beneath the

assault of falling weapons. Had anyone a ruddy
cigarette? Of course not; and his own were soaked
and useless. Did that damned bumping mean 'he'
was coming over? ('He' was the 'Central Powers.')
For Everitt's part, he should 'pack up' if they did,
and he recommended everybody else to do the same.
He was too tired to do anything but curse. He
cursed the rain, the mud, the Germans, the Allies,
the Loamshires, the lice, the rifles, the ammunition,
his friends, his enemies, his Creator, and all things
created. What was the real balance of his emotions
no one knew less than himself. In any emergency
the force of example would doubtless have set him
in common action with the others: there was no
suggestion that he should be summarily shot for
'dispiriting the troops.' For the rest, he was wet,
tired, stiff, dirty, lousy, hungry and cantankerous.

Breakfast consisted of bully-beef, biscuits, bread,
cheese, and jam, all of which were liberally besprin-
kled with mud immediately on disinterment from
the haversacks where they had long been making
merry with socks, rifle oil, towels and soap. The
beef and jam were safe in tins, but the others
emerged in various and unfamiliar disguises. The
meal over, they returned to the futility of cleaning
their rifles. It was impossible to find a spot free
from mud, and a minute after cleaning they were
clogged again. Grit in the bolt of a rifle makes it
entirely useless, save as a peculiarly clumsy club;
but rifles of course were rarely fired in the line. In

the crowded trench the wonder was that no one had the good fortune to be accidentally shot.

Mutual recriminations were disturbed by a call for volunteers to carry ammunition to the forward trench. Everitt knew that any action was better than the idle estimation of the pitch of shells, and that the danger outside was less terrible face to face. With him went his friend Forsyth, ex-Civil Servant, bachelor, and confirmed humorist. His story of the simultaneous surrender of himself and a gigantic Prussian Guardsman is remembered by many to this day — their mutual disappointment and querulous debate, the spinning of a coin to decide the matter, and Forsyth's victorious return with a delighted prisoner. He had just an hour to live, but, not knowing this, his spirits were by no means daunted. Between them they lugged the box by its corded handles. The communication trench ran forward for perhaps two hundred yards, sometimes deep enough for welcome shelter, sometimes so shallow that they seemed gesticulating on a mound. Blocking the road lay some half-dozen dead Fusiliers, killed in yesterday's 'operations.' Many had been thrown out of the trench, wherein they had evidently taken shelter, but upon these six it was impossible to avoid trampling. Each wayfarer thus stamped them further into the mud, and soon their bodies would be hidden. At one place they found a grave. On a fragment of board was scrawled in violet pencil, now smudged by the rain, the name

43

and regiment of him who lay buried there. Humble garden flowers had been brought there to testify the love of friends. A bully-beef tin held them, pansies, cornflowers and coreopsis, gathered God knows where, perhaps dispatched in a parcel from home. This sudden patch of colour in the squalid desert hit them like a blow. So infinitely pitiful seemed those wilting flowers, sodden and drooping in the rain.

At a junction of trenches was a dump of ammunition, and there Everitt first heard the news. All this accumulation of material was for use that afternoon; the battalion was to 'go over' after dinner. Hitherto Everitt had found his creed of confirmed pessimism an actual boon on active service: always prepared for the worst, any alleviation was doubly welcome. But this blank certainty was very different from the nebulous forebodings of half an hour ago. Everitt had had little enough experience, but he knew what 'over the top' meant. Not rarely had he listened to first-hand narratives, and the details had impressed him. Pessimism implies a wilful imagination. Everitt knew only too well that cowards die many deaths. Hence, indeed, his present refuge from thought in action.

But apprehension would not be denied. It had actually come at last. In an hour or so he would be walking eastwards over that field. (It struck him as ludicrous that a man might go east and west together.) A trapped rabbit may be supposed to share his thoughts. He knew he should go with the others; he knew there was no conceivable escape. Unless, indeed, he caught one first. It was a matter of luck after all. Some died and some didn't, and neither skill nor strength nor courage availed a jot to shift Fate's finger. Already he knew enough to know there would be none of the excitement of a 'charge': it would be a slow toiling in the face of machine-guns. Often on the butts at home he had wondered how men dared advance against modern rifles: it seemed incredible that any should survive. At all events he would know all about it soon — perhaps all about everything. If only he had a shred of enthusiasm to support him; if only he could drug himself to believe that this was the right and proper solution of a quarrel. And, talking of drugs, why could he not get drunk on rum? Didn't the Germans dope their men with alcohol?

A mind incurably argumentative saw many sides to every question, most of all to this great problem. How much was there to be said on either side! Certainly they both claimed the support of God and Justice. He was convinced that the men who 'enjoyed the privilege of fighting for their country' were sick of the slaughter, victims driven help-lessly forward by fire-eaters in safe places. Could they not call a truce — and hammer out some settlement? But Germany must be crushed. Ruthless-ness could only be met with ruthlessness. In a little while he himself must be 'ruthless' — he, a physical

45

coward, half convinced that all killing was murder,
hating even the aggression of outdoor games, care-
ful to spare the beetle on the path. It was ludi-
crously impossible that he should grapple with a
German. Perhaps he would encounter a like-minded
foe: he pictured them philosophizing together on
the ethics of the situation. If only it were all over,
and he dead, or wounded, or a prisoner. And so
back to the trench, with normal apprehensions
growing to a numbing dread.

Their news was stale to 'C' Company and for a
time the talk ran on conjectures. It was obvious
that 'A' Company in the forward trench must, in
the barbarous jargon of war, make up the first and
second 'waves,' but against rifle and machine-gun
fire the rear is little better off than the van. They
discussed the vile technicalities of barrages and
the possibilities of a smoke-screen. The wiseacres
declared that going over was nothing to repell-
ing the counter-attacks. Hitherto Everitt had
debated these things academically, after the manner of experts in Pall Mall, and he found it a
very different matter to consider them in the light
of cold facts, affecting him personally and inevitably. To break his sunny musings, there arrived a
fatigue-party of an officer and six men, carrying
bombs from 'D' Company in the rear. They had
started a dozen strong, but some fell by the wayside. 'A rotten job,' some called it, others more
tersely 'a bastard.' An uncommunicative sergeant

distributed the bombs, one for each man, with instructions for their stowage in great-coat pockets. Everitt's chief care was to see that the pin was tightly fixed, and his private resolve was to fling the bomb away at the first opportunity. In any attempt to use the thing offensively it would be just his luck to damage only himself. Certainly this looked like business, and he returned to meditation. Simultaneously he made two discoveries. One was a human arm in a corner of the trench, khaki-clad and neatly severed above the elbow. (The blood had drained away from it and the fractured bone reminded him grotesquely of a knuckle of lamb. The body to which it belonged lay outside the trench ten yards away.) The other was, that this was Sunday, 'the day of rest and gladness, the day of joy and light, the balm of care and sadness, most beautiful, most bright.' At home they were squaring bayonets with the Sermon on the Mount, praying for the safety of loved ones, with roast lamb and green peas as a comforting background. For the owner of that severed arm they were imploring a 'happy issue out of all his afflictions.'

At this moment Higgins emerged from his dug-out. He was ever a man of few words, and his present purpose made brevity necessary. And these were the words of Higgins: 'We go over at 2.45. You'll see "A" Company leave their trench, and all you've got to do is to follow them. Keep some sort of a line, and for God's sake don't bunch. If you do, they'll get you sure as a gun. Just keep your eye on me and follow my direction. Half-way over we've got to swing half-left, but it's only five hundred yards altogether and we ought to get there easily. There's no wire, and you'll find they pack up when we get close. Whatever you do, don't throw bombs about without orders – you'll only hurt your pals if you do, and it won't be necessary. Keep your rifles clean, ten in the chamber and one up the spout.' So that was that, and there still wanted two hours to 'zero.'

Someone said that the objective was, appropriately enough, 'Hazy Trench,' but the news was received without enthusiasm. Apparently the 'blood-lust' was not yet roused, and it was unnecessary to hold back early starters. Orders came down the trench that the men were to make a 'good meal,' and the instruction seemed to them a masterpiece of cynicism. It was absurd to devour food when a few hours might relieve a man from the necessity of any further exertions in that direction. 'Like fattening ducks,' said someone. The old superstition of 'Tempting Providence' raised its head. To build up strength for to-morrow seemed 'asking for it.' Moreover, it was impossible to enjoy bully-beef dug out of a tin with a rusty jack-knife, and the biscuits and cheese made nauseous swallowing. Jam seemed strangely plentiful, and they wolfed it eagerly and undiluted.

The time drifted slowly; self-preservation directed

another oiling of the bolt, but mud mocked men's efforts. Gradually Everitt found himself growing excited. His heart was throbbing unwontedly, and he found himself breathing quickly and swallowing often. He had never believed that a crisis could turn a man's stomach, but evidence was not wanting that some were ill indeed. He himself felt qualms within and a gripping pain that waxed and waned. Talk subsided, but as the time approached cigarettes glowed in larger and larger numbers. Everywhere men were lighting up, puffing and exhaling. It was vitally necessary to do something, and the mere mechanical movements of smoking were a solace. To read was impossible, for thought wandered continually in one direction.

Only half an hour more. Everitt began to believe that a much longer delay would drive him mad. Something whispered to him to start away now, alone. No longer did the tales he had heard of broken nerve seem incredible. He had read of men reduced by fear to trembling jellies of alarm, unable even to stand: others he knew had actually gone crazy.

Another damp cigarette and another futile oiling of the bolt. Suddenly he saw the man beside him reading with apparent absorption a small book bound in calf. Curious to see what could hold a man at such a time, he must needs stoop to read the title: 'Thomas à Kempis! Imitation of Christ!' He knew that Myers was a devout Roman Catholic, and that it was his custom to read a chapter of the 'Imitation' daily. The two were bound together by a love of books. They were chums in the section, and many a time they had drowned their troubles in fierce arguments on Francis Thompson. Religion they had tacitly agreed to exclude from these debates, for a devout Catholic and a pugnacious Agnostic could find little common ground. In Everitt's excuse it may be urged that he was roused to the tensest pitch of anxiety and apprehension. It exasperated him to see a man reading such a book at such a time. To him it savoured of cant. For the life of him he could not help crying: 'What the devil is the good of reading that stuff? Why on earth spend your time that way?' To which Myers replied calmly, 'Why not?' and finished the chapter.

'Get ready,' said someone, and Thomas à Kempis was stowed away for a more convenient season. The cigarettes were glowing more strongly than ever, and a few men shook hands with shamefaced wishes for mutual good luck. Here again Everitt must needs sneer at the imbecility of such sentimentalism. As though it made any difference! But the other recognized the snapping of taut nerves and took compassion on a feeble vessel. Rifles, fully cocked and with fixed swords, were slung over the right shoulder, and each man carried two bandoliers of emergency ammunition. Battle-order had discarded packs. The pouches were left open for use, but up to the last moment Everitt could not believe he should meet any of the enemy hand to hand. The rain fell sullenly, and he saw Higgins pour the contents of his flask into a pannikin and drink it off at a draught. 'Come along,' said he prosaically, and in a minute the trench was empty.

III

I<small>T</small> was a difficult matter to scramble up those slippery banks, and each man stooped to help his neighbour. Every section had been instructed to leave the trench in single file at a chosen point, but, once outside, the whole Company formed a rough alignment. As Everitt straightened himself from helping a friend, he saw 'A' Company emerging from their advanced trench two hundred yards ahead. Their line seemed curiously ragged, but as 'C' Company left their shelter behind them they too gathered themselves into little knots and groups. In a few minutes they were rather in parallel columns than line, and the warning against 'bunching' was unheeded. They had barely left the trench when there rose from the German lines a shower of variegated fireworks — Verey lights, red rockets, green rockets, clustered golden-rains. These were signals to artillery, and in less than a minute the devil's orchestra was in full chorus. From across the valley the barrage fell behind the front line, and so far forward there was little danger from the shelling. But the sudden fierceness and clamour of the guns was awesome to hear, particularly to men primed with tales of the Allies' immeasurable superiority in artillery. Save for intermittent shrapnel fire, no reply came from friendly batteries, and soon even this ceased. Apparently no artillery support

52

was to be given. The 'element of surprise' in a sudden midday attack was thought an ample protection.

Simultaneously with the rockets came the deafening tattoo of rapid fire from rifles and machine-guns. For some distance a fold in the ground gave cover, and, until he reached the farther slope, Everitt saw few casualties. Out there the ground showed patches of green where the winnowing of the shells had spared it. There was no attempt to charge: over such broken ground it was almost impossible to run, and tired men spared their strength. Their greatcoats were clogged with mud, and at every step their boots seized clods of earth: the weight of equipment dragged like an anchor. With slung rifles, and tin hats pressed down over their eyes, they went forward at a plodding walk. Never was there less likelihood of 'running amok with bayonet.'

Everitt exchanged the sickliest of smiles with his neighbours. He saw that their faces were pale and their jaws tight clenched. The advance was maddeningly slow and laborious, and the journey forward seemed interminable. The firing ahead was growing fiercer, and soon seemed to creep round to either flank. 'Enfilade fire of machine-guns is deadly.' A man near Everitt staggered and fell noisily into a shell-hole, curling up like a shot rabbit. There seemed no reason why he should do this, but it was not expedient to pause for questions. Men fell near and far, and sinister obstacles on the ground must be avoided. As they reached the top of the rise, the vicious rattle of the firing seemed to rise to desperation. The 'crack, crack, crack' of the rifles gave not an instant's relief to the ear: in the din the hum of the bullets was inaudible. Against the background of grey sky and glittering rockets the flash of guns showed dimly, but the enemy was invisible.

Beyond the brow of the hill there seemed to be no one advancing. To the left some khaki figures were firing desperately from a fragment of trench, but directly ahead there was no movement. As they crossed the crest men began to fall rapidly all along the line. Everitt and his neighbours flung themselves on the ground, cowering into shell-holes if they were lucky enough to drop near one. 'What do we do now?' asked someone. No one knew and there was no one to give orders. Higgins at least had given his last.

Now was the test of discipline and initiative. The choice lay between organized rushes forward and indefinite delay, and it was not entirely a matter of courage or cowardice; duty or shirking. Against what was evidently overwhelming fire, any advance might well be suicidal folly and in the absence of leadership and encouragement, the law of self-preservation swept aside all discipline: since no one seemed to care what happened, men determined to play their own hands. No doubt that moment of hesitation marked the failure of the attack. Hitherto, while there had never been any pretence of enthusiasm, at least the attempt was being made. Now they were fatally quiescent. It is a commonplace of war that a man who takes cover during an advance will never get up again until the battle is over. Everitt lay as flat as the bulging equipment allowed, and almost immediately felt horribly afraid. While he was walking forward he was doing something and his mind could occupy itself with the details of the advance – the men, the fire signals of the Germans, the lie of the land, the physical labour of covering the broken ground. All these things kept thought away. But now there was nothing to do but think, and the thoughts were black.

He was convinced that the attack was a failure. Lying face downwards, almost biting the earth, he could see nothing, but an occasional upward jerk of his head showed him that all forward movement had ceased completely. The man nearest to him yelled suddenly, 'I'm hit, I'm hit,' and writhed helplessly in the tangle of his equipment. Everitt, feeling himself a cur, dragged himself away into the shallow depression of a small shell-hole. There he lay at first like a log, his nose and mouth pressed into the earth, not daring to raise his head. Then he began to scoop the soil from beneath his body, hoping thus to deepen his shelter. His legs from the knees downwards were hopelessly exposed, but by enlarging the hole he might at least obtain cover from view. The 'crump' from a high explosive shell shook the ground like an earthquake, and a sharp pain stung his foot. But this was the merest momentary pang, like the prick of a needle, and the pain stirred him to fiercer efforts. Involuntarily he called out, 'I've caught one,' but no one took the smallest notice. As he lay he could see the spurt of the earth where bullets were striking, and some of them were pitching not a yard away. His awkward scooping had done little to deepen the hole, and it was obvious that movement was dangerous.

Suddenly there came a tremendous jerk sideways to his left leg, much as though someone had kicked it with a padded boot. The sensation was sickening and numbing rather than painful, and involuntarily he grunted through gritted teeth to keep back a louder cry. The qualm of sickness and surprise passed quickly, and he realized that he was hit. In desperation he glanced sideways at his leg, and saw a red stain soaking through the puttees. But he felt no warm welling of blood and gambled on the safety of the artery. A severed main-artery will kill a man in five minutes, but to sit up and apply a tourniquet was suicide. It was better to leave the wound unbandaged. For the rest, he had no notion whether his leg were broken, and for the moment had not the courage to test his fears.

A machine-gun not two hundred yards away swept the ground in a leisurely traverse, the deliberate 'pop, pop, pop, pop, pop' waxing to deafening sharpness as the fire drew nearer. Again and again the tattoo of the gun rose and fell with the sweep of its traverse, and always, at the zenith of its crescendo, Everitt clenched his teeth and shut his eyes in breathless anticipation of another wound. He had no means of knowing whether the Germans could see him or whether he was the victim of a chance shot. If he lay motionless was he invisible? Or would they think him dead? Perhaps after all they could *not* see him. Above all he must lie still, for it seemed that shots answered his slightest movement.

The man near him lay exposed on a mound of earth, and a body-wound made it impossible for him to roll or crawl to shelter. Twice more he was hit, and still he did not lose consciousness. Moaning and sobbing miserably, with tragic futility he called continually for stretcher-bearers (as though such could live for a moment in the open). 'It hurts so, it hurts so,' he kept crying, a child again in his pain, and soon he was praying to God and his mother to help him. 'Try to get in a hole, chum,' Everitt called to him. His duty was to try to help the other, at least to bandage his wounds and drag him to shelter, but he dared not leave his hole. The bullets continued to raise little spurts of earth around them, and he could do nothing but watch them in frozen fascination.

'Would they hit him again? Where would they get him?' 'That was a near one. If only it would get dark.' Night became a thing to watch for as a possible deliverer. It must be past three o'clock – five or six hours to wait, and then, if he wasn't hit again, and the Germans didn't counter-attack at dusk, it might yet be possible to escape. This was the first faint glow of hope, a determination not to give in, to reach home yet in spite of everything.

He remembered again that this was Sunday. 'P.S.A.,' he murmured, and thought of hymn-singing in church, where the sun filled the air with the smell of warm varnish. No doubt his father was dozing after dinner in his easy chair, with mouth agape and waistcoat unbuttoned. Outside the bees were busy with the flowers, and the cat was sleeping in the sunshine. What a fool he was to be there — what fools they all were. There were a hundred ways of avoiding this horror, and what was the good of it all? Thousands of men were lying crumpled in those fields, helpless, agonized, hopeless, frozen with terror, tortured with wounds. Blind fate slew them and spared them and death came often as a boon. And now the horror continued and grew greater, and more men were struck minute by inexorable minute. The bullets fell impartially on earth and flesh, and the maddening clamour of the machine-guns showed no sign of slackening. Moans, prayers, curses, entreaties, inarticulate cries, the stench of mud and blood and fumes and smoke, the thunder of guns, the shriek of shells and the rattle of rifle-fire, a chill rain soaking unchecked into that medley of woe — a modern battlefield! And fools talk of the glory of war, and the joy of battle! 'The lordliest life on earth!'

Perhaps Everitt was growing light headed, for abruptly his thoughts jerked in another direction. Was it any use to pray? He had heard in a dozen sermons that in extremity the stoutest atheist would pray for help to the God he denied. The parsons assured him that freethinker and agnostic joined with the most devout believer in instinctive supplication: the fact was stated as a final buttress of belief. But his actual experience was different. With men dead and dying on every side it was impossible to believe that God cared. Obviously He did not help the sufferers, call they never so poignantly. 'Either he is talking, or he is pursuing, or he is in a journey, or peradventure he sleepeth, and must be awaked.' How could the paltry individual expect a private miracle in his own behoof? The age of such things was past: the text of consolation: 'A thousand shall fall at thy side, and ten thousand at thy right hand, but it shall not come nigh thee' was applicable only to spiritual experience, which, under present circumstances, made it a little inadequate. In point of fact it meant nothing at all. The healing solace of prayer as an instinctive exercise of the soul seemed more than a little at a discount. Everitt wanted help, and he received none.

This cannot be put on one side as the flippant disclaimer of the prosperous fool – untouched by misfortune and proportionately puffed up – the man was in deadly peril, in anguish of mind and body. Never had he felt less reason for intellectual pride.

By a curious mental twist, he felt impelled to shape in his thoughts a statement of belief. Let the stress of the time be the excuse for its inadequacy. 'A personal God may exist; there is no evidence of His existence, but ignorance cannot deny it. But, if He does, He cares nothing for the fate of individuals. Men are "tossed down into the field," and left to the blind disposal of natural laws. These sequences of cause and effect leave him no room for "free-will." Traced to its source, his every action is an automatic reaction to external influences. In ignorance of these causes, he calls his vicissitudes "Chance," for any event, originating outside his experience, is necessarily fortuitous to reason. The God of Earth and Heaven by no means interferes arbitrarily with these natural laws, and in themselves these laws are impersonal, rigid, and without mercy. I can do nothing to help myself and the misty God of the Christians will do nothing to help me. If the path of a bullet passes through my brain I shall die. In the contrary event, I shall live.'

It was difficult to keep count of time (his watch had been broken long ago), but at the end of the longest hour of his life the firing showed signs of abating. Soon there was no doubt of it. Now it came in gusts, and gradually the continuous roar died away to sniping. But it was well he remained quiet, for, after perhaps another hour, the firing swelled out again to all its original fury. The old nerve-shaking suspense clutched him again, and the spurts of earth showed death searching and capricious. A sudden jab in his left elbow and a numbing pain after the manner of a jarred funny-bone must be another wound. Everitt could not help muttering 'Number three,' though with but a twisted grin, and it seemed hopeless that his luck could hold much longer.

The renewed firing was occasioned by the advance of another line of khaki from the trench behind. These were men of the Loamshires from 'D' Company in support. It was evident that part at least of the battalion had gained some kind of objective, and that these happy warriors were intended to stiffen the defence. Everitt risked looking up at them, and feebly croaked 'stick it,' as they passed. The face of a man advancing against machine-guns is not good to see. Shell-fire can be regarded as haphazard at the worst, but a machine-gun in an attack fires almost point-blank at a very definite target. The men walked slowly, just as he had done, stumbling forward with a sort of dogged hopelessness, wincing and blinking in dread of a bullet. As far as he could see, for all their hopelessness there was no tendency to give up. It was a miracle that so few were hit.

The glare of a Verey light roused Everitt from a kind of stupor, and he found to his surprise that it was dusk. Either he had slept or fainted, and it must now be eight o'clock. It was an indescribable relief to know that the time of inaction was passed, and the glow of hope burned more brightly. He had survived the attack, and surely the worst was behind him. As soon as it was dark, venturing to sit up and look about him, he was startled to find that of all those who had thrown themselves down around him only some half-dozen remained, and that these lay motionless and silent. Evidently the others had risked everything to obtain some kind of shelter.

His first business was to examine his leg. To his great joy he found that he could move it freely without pain: evidently a simple flesh wound that had not yet had time to stiffen. Sitting upright, his next care was to tear off his equipment, and fling his bomb as far from him as he was able. This abandonment he marked as the first faint turning of the tide: never had a man fewer qualms in the surrender of property. He was getting rid of hated encumbrances and realized for the first time, and with a kind of fearful joy, that no one could blame him, and that, howsoever helpless, he was his own master until he should reach an ambulance.

And this brought home to him how far away help was, and how doubtful his chances. With a sinking heart he remembered the infinite toil of the journey to the line. How could he hope to reach even the trench, much less the road? He must see if he could find anyone to help him. It was a starry night, and within a circuit of perhaps twenty yards he could see some dozen motionless and contorted bodies. The gloom hid other horrors doubtless, but a faint and intermittent groaning showed that some at least of these muddy bundles yet held tortured life within them. The man who had been hit three times was still conscious, panting for breath, but speechless from exhaustion.

Everitt's effort to stand upright showed that his leg, if unbroken, yet thrilled with pain when weight was placed upon it. It seemed that it must snap at the least pressure, and he noticed that the contracting muscles had drawn the heel upwards until only the toes could touch the ground. Evidently he could not walk unaided.

Help was imperative, and instinctively he thought of Myers. He had forgotten his existence for half a dozen hours, but weakness quickened his affection. In dread of the enemy he dared not raise his voice above a whisper, but almost immediately one of the motionless figures rose to its feet and blundered clumsily towards him. (But in no-man's-land at night every man has the gait of a drunkard.) A flare, however, revealed the cause of the figure's staggering, and at the same time showed that it was Myers.

But a Myers strangely altered! Round his head was a field-bandage, black with congealed blood, and an ominous wine-coloured crust concealed his face. From the edge of the roughly tied bandage the blood had dripped and hardened into grotesque black stalactites. Beneath its stains his face showed white and ghastly. 'Caught a whack from shrapnel,' he whispered. 'Knocked me silly for some time, and at first I thought I was done for. Just as though my head had been split. It's throbbing like the devil and I'm as giddy as a goose. What's yours?'

Everitt explained, and together they tied a field-dressing to his leg. The muddy puttee was tightly glued to the flesh beneath, but persistent effort removed it to reveal a neat plum-coloured patch on either side of the calf. His arm was stiffening and they despaired of releasing it from the sleeves of great-coat and tunic.

All at once they discovered that they were parched with thirst, and in a minute their two water-bottles were empty. Immediately there arose from every side that terrible litany of the wounded: 'A drink, for Christ's sake.' Myers seemed to be the only man capable of walking, and he did the only thing possible – took their bottles from the dead and gave them to the living. He also produced a flat circular tin of malted milk lozenges ('Meat and drink together,' said the advertisement) and these the scarecrows munched together with huge satisfaction. After a time they saw not far away the dim shapes of men digging, and heard the sound of smothered English curses. In a little while someone came over to them – a man of the Loamshires – to be instantly assailed with two demands – 'Stretcher-bearers' and 'the time.' But of neither could he tell anything very definite. 'It might be about ten o'clock, and no doubt there are stretcher-parties at work. You'll be all right soon, but we can't leave off our job to help you chaps just now. Anyhow, we've got no stretchers.' Thus the

64

visitor – a melancholy man with a disillusioned air, for which perhaps he had ample reason.

It seemed that the remnants of the battalion were 'digging-in' not two hundred yards from the front enemy trench. The attack had reached the Germans 'in places,' but the isolated fragments of trench so captured were untenable and had been abandoned in the darkness. No one knew exactly either where he was or where was the enemy. To-morrow they expected counter-attacks. 'God knows what will happen, and He won't split.' More than half the battalion were casualties, and they looked like receiving neither water nor rations. There were rumours of relief to-morrow night, but in the meantime every one was 'fed up and beat to the wide.' With this benediction the visitor left them, vaguely promising to 'hurry up the stretcher-bearers.'

This dispiriting news made Everitt more anxious than ever to make an effort to regain the trench. In the darkness the place now seemed swarming with troops, and it was extraordinary that an enemy, who could not be more than a quarter of a mile away, made no attempt to disturb them. Yet the murmuring and thudding and clinking of the working parties met with no interruption, and mutual suspicion and uncertainty produced a truce. It was more than ever imperative, however, to gain some kind of shelter, and the muddy ditch they had left so unwillingly eight hours earlier now seemed to Everitt and Myers a kind of City of Refuge.

They reckoned that they had not more than three hundred yards to cover, and it was to be expected that some kind of organized help would be available in the trench. 'What about these others?' said Myers, voicing both their thoughts. 'We can't do anything for them, and the stretcher-bearers will be along soon,' answered Everitt, who, truth to tell, cared for one thing only – to leave that patch of ground which he already realized he should see in his mind's eye to his dying day. But the others heard their talk, and with the wounded man's pathetic anxiety for company, begged and beseeched them not to leave them. 'Don't go away, chum, don't leave us here. Can't you help any way at all? I'm sure I could get along if you'd only help,' – when some of them could not even sit upright. 'Poor old Jimmy's hit through the lungs,' said Myers; 'he won't last long.' Jimmy lay only a little way off, choking and coughing, and choking again. 'How goes it, chum?' 'Pretty bad, mate,' and further words were drowned in a mouthful of blood. As well as they could they propped his head against a haversack and wrapped round him his great-coat and waterproof sheet. Myers had bandaged the wound ('both lungs, poor devil – not an earthly'), and a drink of water was all they could do for him in parting. 'Good luck, Jimmy – they'll soon pick you up.' 'Good luck, Tom, you'll be in Blighty in a week,' and a choking cough followed them into the darkness. Jim Frampton, a gentle, peace-loving countryman, they had both known from the day they had enlisted together, and, as they stumbled away, they felt like traitors, and almost murderers. Yet, to stay there was merely uselessly to imperil their own chances. Cruel as it seemed to leave the others behind them, there was nothing they could do for them. 'Perhaps they'll be carried off to-night by the stretcher-bearers,' said Everitt, but he knew the folly of any such delusion. For a battalion has only sixteen stretchers at best, adequate perhaps to holding the line, but absurdly insufficient in present circumstances. It would take two men at least three hours to carry a loaded stretcher to the road and an hour to return; there were perhaps four hundred casualties in the battalion; the survivors were working on the new trench-line throughout the night; what were Frampton's chances? Everitt never saw him again, and later counted his name among the killed.

At first Everitt tried to crawl, but the uneven ground twisted his injured leg unbearably. Then he attempted a kind of grotesque shuffle in a sitting position, stretching his left leg stiffly ahead and working himself forward by his hands. But by this means progress was painfully slow and infinitely exhausting, and it proved impossible to preserve under such circumstances the least sense of direction. Myers could obviously have found his way easily enough, but it seemed never to occur to him to do so. At last they pooled their resources. Using his rifle, barrel downwards, as a kind of

crutch, Everitt threw his uninjured arm round
Myers' neck and, thus locked together in a drunkard's embrace, they steered a twisted course westwards. It was a partnership in infirmities. Everitt,
helplessly lame, found a clear head and a keen pair
of eyes; Myers, dizzy and partially blinded, sup-
plied the motive power. Every hole and ridge was
a trap, and a dozen times in five minutes they fell
headlong. Again and again they must pause and
rest, and in one such respite Everitt in vain attempted to propound an epigram that might be
worthy of the occasion. But he tried in vain. It
was no time for wit, and sarcasm must wait for
safety.

Despite their snail's progress all sound of the
working party died behind them. Snipers' rifles
cracked like whips through the silence, and always
the cold white flares were rising and falling. Overhead stray shells moaned and rumbled continually,
but the zone of their danger lay far to the rear. They
steered entirely by the Verey lights, aiming always
to leave them behind, but finding, after the manner
of traffickers in no-man's-land, that the flares rose
obstinately on three sides of them. Now and again
they passed dead men, men of the Loamshires side
by side with Fusiliers, and once clay upon clay beside
a riven thorn-bush. This bush Everitt thought he
remembered, and they were encouraged to greater
efforts.

But the intense exertion of their journey sent the

sweat from them in salt streams, and soon their throats were dry as kilns. Once more they must rob the dead. Twice they drew blank, but the third attempt yielded a bottle nearly full of lemonade, made that morning with powder sent from home. 'He likes lemonade so much.' And now strangers were drinking it, and they knew nothing, and he lay staring at the stars. The tang of the drink restored them and again they struggled onwards.

After a time Everitt felt himself so ill that he begged Myers to go ahead while he rested. In ten minutes the latter returned triumphantly. He had discovered a trench, not a hundred yards distant, occupied by men of a Rifle battalion, who, with the characteristic haziness of the 'forward area,' had told him they 'rather thought they were holding the front line.' At all events they knew nothing of any occupied trench to their front. It seemed that the Loamshire's original position lay farther to the left in this same trench, and that the Riflemen formed a flanking battalion to the attack. The whole position was incredibly hazy. For all they knew the Germans might be sharing the trench with them, and the revealing dawn might involve an instant struggle. But such a state of things was inherent to the forward fringe of the Push, and in the meantime the Riflemen were anxious chiefly for rum.

Thus advised, Myers had walked along the trench leftwards until he found a dump of wounded in charge of two stretcher-bearers. These were all

Loamshire men, who told him that the casualties were being collected there until some arrangement could be made for their removal by carrying-parties. This news brought him back hot foot to Everitt, whom, since all sense of direction was lost in an instant in so trackless a wilderness, he only found after five minutes' hoarse shouting and stumbling into holes. A last effort carried them to the lip of the trench, to which arose mysterious whispers from utter darkness. Letting himself slide as gently as might be over the parapet, Everitt found himself caught safely in the arms of invisible strangers and stowed forthwith recumbent on a muddy fire-step. There were several wounded men lying on the floor of the trench, but the gloom gave no idea of their number. Wrapped in great-coat and ground-sheet, Everitt was exhausted enough to be careless even whether there was any chance of further progress. He fell asleep instantly, and it was bright daylight when he awoke.

At once his thoughts turned to breakfast. Once again Myers' famous lozenges were alone available, and their ravenous neighbours shared in the feast. (Here was material for a notable advertisement, entirely wasted in the absence of a camera.) The stretcher-bearers had disappeared in the darkness, and the talk turned solely on what was next to do. All save Myers were so badly hurt that walking was out of the question, and the Guillemont road seemed infinitely remote. As the sun climbed higher, thirst grew upon them, and the flies, banished by yester-day's wet weather, resumed their loathsome visita-tions. Evidently nothing could be done until dusk; and they must resign themselves to a further twelve hours' meditation. As far as Everitt was concerned, so long as he lay motionless, his leg gave him no pain, but he avoided instinctively the smallest move-ment. Words were few in the hot stuffiness of the trench, and hunger and thirst made it easy to quarrel. At last someone found a muddy *Royal Magazine*, and the treasure was divided into eight fragments. But reading made the men sleepy, and their thoughts flew continually towards possibilities of escape. Also the haphazard rationing of the book had been effected regardless of literary continuity. The crux of a story was invariably in a neighbour's hands.

For four hours no one came near them, but about eleven o'clock the two stretcher-bearers returned with heaven-sent rations of bread, jam, cheese, and bully-beef, together with full water-bottles. Jack-knives and fingers made short work of the food, which was wolfed by ravenous men as though it were the choicest meal in the world. Everitt's arm was now so stiff that he was unable to bend the elbow, and his one-handed manœuvres left him hideously bedaubed with jam and grease.

Hunger satisfied, they besieged their benefactors with questions. 'How did we get on yesterday?' 'Where's the batt.?' and above all 'How are we going to get away?' But the good samaritans had no definite news. (They seemed doomed to a limbo of Rumour.) The rations they had obtained from a Company of the Rifles near by. Evidently units were hopelessly mixed, and all they could learn of the Loamshires was that they were 'out in front somewhere.' Every one asked in chorus whether the Rifles would carry them out, but the stretcher-bearers could tell them nothing. It was indeed all too probable that other battalions would be fully occupied with their own affairs.

At length the bearers disappeared again, ostensibly to 'have a look round,' perhaps to make arrangements for the evening. With their going Everitt fell helplessly into black depression. It seemed to him that they were marooned in that narrow trench indefinitely – isolated, forgotten, cut off alike from friend and foe. Among that helpless knot of strangers, gathered haphazard from the storm outside, it was easy to believe that the ordered machine of the army had no longer any concern with them. Why hadn't they been carried away last night? Why should it be any more feasible to-night – or any other night? Suppose the Germans came over. They were utterly helpless and hopelessly exposed. Who knew what would happen before nightfall, or for the matter of that, after it? What were stretchers and stretcher-bearers for?

All this, in place of thankfulness for so many dangers cheated, and the miracle of their survival inducing no optimism for the future! Yet, to their jangled nerves, this ebb of courage seemed perfectly natural, and shame came only long afterwards. Everitt remained obstinately pessimistic, and refused to be comforted by any argument. To all and sundry he replied that they were 'in the cart.'

Thus, quarrelling, dozing, reading, and dozing again, the long hours dragged slowly towards the evening. No one visited them: every scrap of food and drink was gone: they were unable to raise even a cigarette between them. And, as Myers said, if the Angels of Mons should appear to him that moment, the only manna he would ask would be a 'Woodbine.' One thing seemed to Everitt extraordinary. Not a Chaplain had he seen since he was wounded. This was notoriously out of keeping with tradition. Every one knew that no-man's-land during an attack swarmed with Chaplains, administering consolation spiritual and spirituous, and picking up Military Crosses like so many gooseberries. Everitt's experience of these men of God must have been exceptional, for he never saw one of them in front of reserve trenches, and associated them chiefly with Concert Parties and Church Parades. A gramophone was the sole social stock in trade of the Loamshire's Chaplain. He would deposit this instrument among the men's bivouac when they were out 'resting,' and lounge near it, smiling foolishly while it blared brazen versions of 'Roses are blooming in Picardy,' and 'Colonel Bogie.' For the rest, he made an occasional point of asking men 'how they were getting on,' and, receiving only colourless and embarrassed answers, retired with obvious relief to the more civilized shelter of the officers' mess. There at least he would find whisky and bridge and the conversation of educated men. On the not infrequent occasions when the Battalion's daily duties called it into unpleasant localities, the reverend and gallant gentleman was less in evidence. What he did no one seemed to know. Rumour declared he pressed the Colonel's trousers, but more probably he merely laid low like Br'er Rabbit. At long last he was trepanned by a fire-eating Colonel into a burial party in front of Ypres, and immediately afterwards returned to England for a prolonged rest. But doubtless Everitt's experience was exceptional and unfortunate.

In a traversed trench, where a man can never see ten yards in any direction, a new-comer must needs arrive without warning, and there now appeared with sufficiently dramatic suddenness a visitor more welcome than any number of chaplains or angels. This was Lieutenant Mackie, thin, pale, keen-eyed and sarcastic. A Distinguished Conduct Medal for once summarized the man who wore it. Only yesterday he had persisted in promenading the line while the shelling was hottest, scattering chaff on the tremblers in the trench below. Call this unnecessary, foolhardy; Gascon bravado; yet it was good to see and mightily heartening. It was this same Mackie

who later lost his adjutancy by indulging, under the
stimulus of rum, and clad only in pyjamas, in un-
seemly gestures on the parapet in the moonlight.
But that is another story.

On this occasion he came as an angel of light.
'How are you chaps getting on? Rough house, eh!
You'll be out of it to-night; stretcher-bearers will be
on the job soon after dark. Keep the home fires
burning! So long.' You may say that this was
theatrical, and self-consciously melodramatic, but it
was the very thing to raise dashed spirits. Everitt
had the grace to wallow in shame of his cowardice,
and conversation flourished on the fertile theme of
Mackie's adventures. Soon the stretcher-bearers
returned with orders that all wounded must move a
dozen bays down the trench towards the Riflemen. It
seemed that the stretcher-party that night had ap-
pointed a rendezvous at a point where a track from the
road crossed the trench, and there were further sug-
gestions that the near neighbourhood of friends would
prove desirable in certain unspecified eventualities.
The hint was enough, and since Myers could walk,
he was the first to leave. For twenty-four hours
Everitt saw no more of him, and then only for a
moment, but six months later they met again in their
reserve battalion in England, where it was a terrible
joy to live that day again in memory. To his friend's
utter confusion and indignation Everitt ever afterwards regarded him as his preserver, and indeed it
is hard to say how he could have reached the trench

unaided. Such is the whirligig of war that Everitt's last news of him told of his elevation to the dignity of Assistant Town Major of Mons. At the same epoch Everitt had attained to the sole custody of a particularly foul incinerator.

One by one the men disappeared round the traverse, and soon it was Everitt's turn. There were no stretchers, and without them two men were unable to carry a third, but in any event the sharp angles of the trench would have made their use dangerous. First he attempted to crawl, and next he essayed hopping, but the clinging mud making this impossible, he made use of a nameless form of progress dependent on a foot and elbow wedged into the side of the trench. This at first answered better, but soon the banks of the ditch sloped outwards, and the wider space mocked his efforts. Also in places where the parapet was low, any such gymnastics involved exposure. His final plan was to sit down on the floor of the trench, facing his destination, and to work himself forward by a series of thrusts with his hands, the injured leg held stiffly aloft to avoid injury. The bearers followed slowly, lending ineffectual aid.

The procession must have made an amazing spectacle, but at the time the joke was hard to savour. The distance cannot have been more than a quarter of a mile, but, such was the exertion of these unusual acrobatics, that he reached journey's end utterly spent. Breathless and bathed in sweat, he seemed to spend hours in propelling himself round the muddy traverses, and, when at last he was suffered to rest, exhaustion left him for some time like a log.

The new stretch of trench was exactly like the other, and once more the little company settled down to wait for nightfall. The Rifles, it seemed, were only a few bays distant now, but none of them came near. By this time it was afternoon, and the stretcher-party was due at eight o'clock. Only another half-dozen hours!

The time dragged more and more heavily, but at dusk the monotony was rudely broken. Someone suggested that 'the guns were waking up a bit,' and in less than five minutes the whole line was under heavy fire. Whizz-bangs skimmed the trench, sending down showers of earth as they scraped the parapet. The shells came with the sudden venom of lightning. It seemed to Everitt that Fate was playing with them, and that it was only in cruel caprice that they had been permitted to escape thus far. What was that 'Cat and Mouse Act' at home? It has never been agreed whether the last turn of the rack consists in 'going over' or holding out under a bombardment. Certainly the latter ordeal implies a greater helplessness, and on this occasion the victims could not even move a yard towards an imaginary shelter. Shrinking to the floor of the ditch, it was impossible to avoid visualizing the effect of a shell. All of them had had experience of a direct hit among closely packed men, and the sight is not to be easily forgotten. Everitt in

particular ever held his most dreadful memory to
be the appearance of a concrete block-house after a
high explosive shell had actually passed through the
door and exploded among six men. The walls were
splashed with blood and brains, and the victims were
torn to tatters of cloth and flesh that for a few minutes
writhed dumbly in the smoke and dust of the
explosion. And a weak will saw the sight again
continually.

Soon some pessimist chose to ask what was the
cause of the 'bumping,' and at once everybody suspected it to be cover or preparation for an attack.
Dusk is the plausible time for a raid, and they were
miserably conscious of the empty trench on their
left. Suppose the Germans reached it and bombed
their way round the traverses towards the Rifles.
Wounded men could expect little mercy in a hand-
to-hand fight, and a blindly thrown grenade makes
no discrimination. Unanimously they asked the
stretcher-bearers whether they ought not to move
nearer to the Rifles, and in their trepidation even
suggested that some of the latter should occupy the
unguarded trench. But their guardians were optimistic – 'it's only an evening hate – you're safe as
houses. Our boys are just round the corner. This
bumping'll wash out in ten minutes.' In point of
fact it did, but their fears were not entirely groundless.

With darkness the shelling slackened to desultory
shooting from the howitzers, and their spirits rose as

the shattering explosions moved slowly away to the rear. Followed the calm of night-time, rarely broken by the crack of a rifle, and lit always by the rising, hovering, falling radiance of the Verey lights. Excitement grew vivid as seven o'clock crawled towards eight. In less than an hour they would be actually on the way 'out,' and the journey through the shelled line of communications might well be regarded as the last of their troubles. It would doubtless be a trying passage, but at least it would be progress towards a world where men walked upright and unafraid, where trees and houses stood unbroken, where there were other interests than death and wounds. Only thirty hours had passed since they had been wounded, but it seemed many days since they had seen a normal world. The thought that perhaps after all they might reach it again unloosed all tongues, and, perhaps to drown forebodings of that shelled track across the fields, every one fell to discussing their hopes of the base and Blighty. One man with a broken leg grinned appreciation of the congratulations of the others that he would spend Christmas in England. The less-fortunate less-injured men regarded him almost angrily as unjustly favoured, and secretly hoped that their wounds too would prove severe enough to reach the base at least. Someone said that the field-hospitals must needs be jammed with casualties from the Push and that the field-ambulances and Corps clearing-stations were used purely as evacuation-centres for all save desperate cases requiring instant operation. Here was the advantage of a 'lively' front. On a quiet section all save what were euphemistically known as 'long jobs' were retained in the net of the clearing-station, where the ample supply of beds made it possible to cure many a premature optimist. But in the crowded stream of a 'Push,' the necessity of keeping the field-hospitals free from congestion was a golden key to the base, where the same good fortune sometimes worked further miracles. And to crown these rosy dreams came pat the stretcher-party.

IV

In default of lowering the stretchers into the narrow trench, they were laid flat on the ground over against the edge of the parados. Everitt's turn came early. It was a grotesque performance, with one leg useless and a stiff arm, but in a breathless minute he had scrambled from the shadow of the trench into the moonlight. Lying flat upon the stretcher, a folded great-coat made a pillow. No one suggested delay, and forthwith the journey started. Even then Everitt was beginning to look upon it as a stage on the road to London.

The night was cool, and clear, with a brilliant moon and a multitude of stars. The Germans lay not half a mile away across perfectly open country, and it was well for the party to move as rapidly as possible. Four men carried the stretchers, but the maze of craters and the dazzle of the flares made the going irksome; moreover the weight of even the lightest man is a considerable load for four strong bearers. Progress was cruelly slow, and occasionally a man's stumbling tilted the stretcher until Everitt with difficulty kept himself from falling. It was an eerie sensation to be thus carried through the night. The guns gave tongue only intermittently, and the staccato crack of the rifles and machine-guns broke the uncanny silence but rarely. The other parties were lost in the night, and from a probably misplaced dread of being overheard, no one spoke above a whisper. Their language naturally was lurid, and what their curses lost in volume they gained in bitterness. Hoisted high upon the shoulders of four men, Everitt felt himself tremendously conspicuous, and, in the radiance of the Verey lights, it seemed incredible that the whole party was not clearly visible. From his swaying platform nothing was to be seen save a dead world of desolation. It was easy to believe that he was asleep, and that this was the landscape of a fantastic dream.

In accordance with tradition, at every nearer flare the bearers remained motionless, sometimes erect in picturesque silhouette, more often lowering the stretcher, and passing the brief respite in whispered and comprehensive anathemas. Once a machine-gun seemed to fire directly at them, and the soft whizz of the bullets passed apparently close to their ears. It was impossible and perhaps superfluous to know how near the shots were passing, or to discover whether they were being deliberately fired upon, but it seemed best to lie motionless. Everitt, for one, was too badly scared to risk the feeblest remark, and yet he realized what a masterpiece Bairnsfather would have made of the occasion.

Then up again, with Everitt's consciousness of exposure tremendously strengthened! As they left the trench farther behind them, they reached the

region of dropping bullets. Several times they took
cover in holes, the stretcher tilting awkwardly in
the tumbled earth, and twice Everitt was spilled
outright as the men stooped too suddenly for
shelter.

But, thanks to the moon, progress was far speedier
than he had dared hope. At one point indeed they
were held up in the shelter of a low ridge that seemed
to be swept by machine-gun-fire coming from no
one knew where, and, when at length they crossed
it at a stumbling trot, he held his breath with strained
ears. By good fortune they passed the place in safety,
and perhaps his fears were largely imaginary. For
some time Everitt lost his bearings with his courage,
but in just under an hour the party reached some
batteries of 'eighteen pounders' which he remembered must be about half-way to the road. Here
they met men of a relieving battalion 'going up,'
and, contrary to tradition, Everitt's account of the
conditions 'up there' was not encouraging. Certainly he was tired and frayed to distraction, but
every reader of optimistic special correspondents
knows that the wounded are 'wonderfully cheerful.'
Yet it seemed absurd to paint Les Bœufs as rather a
joke, and perhaps an abortive attack conveys to
its survivors on the whole rather the greyer side of
war. At all events Everitt must needs let the new-
comers know what they might expect up yonder,
and he felt a hopeless pity for them when he heard
they were to 'have a cut at Hazy Trench to-morrow.'

It seemed these men of the Oakshires were relieving Everitt's battalion, and the stretcher-party was
at last confirmed in the vague report it had brought
from headquarters. The new-comers were good
fellows and shared with the party the contents of
a whole precious water-bottle. Someone produced
a cigarette – just one 'Woodbine' – which Everitt
received as by divine right. He felt himself a cur
to accept such a treasure – a greater sacrifice to
the donor than anyone could realize who had never
shared the occasion – and for the first time had
an inkling of the privileges of a 'casualty.' Words
are feeble tools to describe the joy of that three
minutes' smoke. At such times as these frayed
nerves shriek for tobacco. Ever afterwards he could
relish the taste of that cigarette, the puff and
pause and exhalation, the scent of the smoke, the
glow of the red ash before it fell. It was good to
know they were far enough back for smoking to be
permissible. The others, poor fellows, had no cigarettes, and doubtless cursed their luck, if silently,
no less fervently. Remember they were carrying
the smoker 'out,' perhaps to Blighty, while they
would remain indefinitely. Yet all they said was,
'Lucky devil!'

Continuing their journey, they crossed a deep
trench that Everitt remembered by reason of a
peculiarly aggravating fall he had made there into
slimy darkness. But the mud had dried after a hot
day, and in the moonlight it was far easier to nego-

tiate. This marked another stage in the journey. They were going down-hill now, and the Verey lights rose but a little way above the ridge behind them. Also they rejoiced in the consciousness of men and guns between them and the enemy. Certainly the worst was passed.

Another hour's journey brought them to a group of dug-outs, where they found scattered fragments of the Loamshires. One and all were disciples of Mr. Micawber. This was 'support,' and here was battalion headquarters and the regimental aid-post. Under normal circumstances it is the duty of the Medical Officer of a battalion in the line to examine all casualties in his unit, administering first-aid and dispatching them rearwards with some kind of pass-port tied to their clothing. (Naturally these 'chits' are prized above rubies.) But that night the majority of the Loamshires were casualties, and there was no attempt to meddle with the wounded. The party halted for some time on the strength of a rumour that the field-ambulance men were carrying from the aid-post to the advanced dressing-station on the road. The M.O. confined himself to wandering half heartedly from stretcher to stretcher (and there were many), asking men if they were 'all right,' and passing on before they had had time to answer. And, indeed, in the darkness, and with practically no shelter, he could do no more.

After half an hour two R.A.M.C. men appeared. They had a party working on the road to the dressing-station, but the battalion bearers must carry on for another half-mile. This was a bombshell to tired men who were expecting relief from a burden they must have hated. A sergeant asked Everitt if he could manage to walk to the road, and two of the men offered to help him. With his fit arm round the neck of one and supported by both, he attempted some kind of shuffling progress, but, the wounded leg proved useless and exquisitely painful. Everitt, in disgust at the infinity of trouble he was causing, offered to stay where he was until daylight, when 'someone will pick me up,' but the four men, hiding their disappointment under cheerful curses at the expense of the R.A.M.C., shouldered their burden once again, and carried it over the remainder of the wilderness between headquarters and the road.

It was an enormous relief to reach even so battered a relic of civilization. How long ago was it that he had left it behind him as the boundary of a habitable world he might never see again? A stretcher-dump by the wayside gave promise of an organized system of evacuation, and the very presence of a road suggested welcome company and traffic after the emptiness of the dreary desolated fields. The bearers laid the stretcher in the mud beside the roadside ditch, and wishing him 'Good luck' shambled away towards Guillemont. If ever men had earned gratitude it was they, yet Everitt could only mumble the heartlessly inadequate:

'Thanks awfully' of his nation, received as inevitably
with: 'Not a bit of it.'

Every such journey is one long series of risks to
all concerned. The slow progress and the impos-
sibility of taking quick cover add immeasurably to
its dangers, and the temptation to abandon the
helpless cause of the trouble is often wellnigh irre-
sistible. That night they had been unusually lucky,
for the spasmodic shelling had never been within
twenty yards of them, and the rifle-fire had been
negligible. More often to the physical exertion of
the journey is added the imminent fear of death.
Yet, in any event, stretcher-bearing is the most
exhausting task on active service. At the end of a
spell a man is commonly dripping with sweat without, bone-dry within, and so exhausted that he can
sleep in his equipment in the adjacent mud. It is
all a commonplace of the line. Everybody does it,
everybody curses it, and everybody, despite the
most desperate extremes of toil and danger, carries
the job through to the end, knowing that he too
may one day lie helpless and in need of the same
succour.

Lying prone in the road, Everitt's chief fear
was that a careless wanderer would tread upon him
in the darkness. Several times the catastrophe
nearly occurred, but he at length grew so sleepy
that he could no longer concern himself with
trifles. Six-inch howitzers were stationed beside the
road – the mud preventing their ponderous weight

leaving it – and almost overhead their deafening uproar split the night continually. The remorseless flash and din of their firing was maddening enough to a man wellnigh hopeless of peace: it seemed to Everitt he would never again be out of their hearing. Nevertheless, he must have slept in spite of them, for a familiar voice roused him.

The Loamshires had been relieved and the survivors were moving back to 'reserve.' In the gloom he could see nothing plainly, but there was evidently no attempt at any sort of order and discipline. They were merely a forlorn mob of weary men dragging themselves doggedly through the mud, half asleep, silent for the most part, continually stumbling against each other, forming and reforming into fortuitous groups of friends and strangers. The voice was Mason's, a man of Everitt's platoon. He had no definite news of anyone, and all he could say of Sunday afternoon was that 'the whole thing was a bloody wash-out.' They were out now, anyway, and had been promised a rest. In any case there were so few of them that a further stay in the line was impossible. The relief, too, was of another Division, which spelled a week or two of peace. 'But you could never tell what might happen.' Attracted by their voices, a third man joined them. This was Tubby Staunton, platoon runner and famous for plum-cake from home. He thought he had seen several of their mutual friends go over,

but he too had no certain news. In the morning
they would be able to count their losses, but by
then Everitt hoped to be far away. Mason gave
him a cigarette (the way to Heaven must be paved
with the Ashes of Woodbines), wished him good
luck, and became another ship that had passed in
the night. Everitt never saw him again, and for the
worst of reasons.

Several times parties of men approached from
the rear, and each time toiled slowly back beneath
laden stretchers. The place seemed to be the
Ultima Thule of the Red Cross: towards the line
a deserted road led through darkness and hidden
horrors towards Bapaume. It was strange to imagine
it crossing the last British outpost line, threading
no-man's-land, passing the successive lines of enemy
trenches, and then growing stable and civilized
again beneath an alien traffic. Everitt tried not to
be impatient, but he could not help asking how
long he must await his turn. 'Not long, chum –
only a few minutes, now,' was the answer, and
unreasonably he cursed the R.A.M.C. as sluggards.
At the back of his mind perhaps were memories of
interminable marches, where men fainted in the
dust, and rest-billets were always 'only another
kilo.'

These men had been carrying for three days and
nights with the briefest intervals for sleep and food;
yet, such is human vanity on the unlikeliest occasions that he forthwith called to mind almost with

self-congratulation that it was the 'foot sloggers' alone who knew the ultimate horror of war. Here shells were rare and the chances incalculably against misfortune, while 'up there' the reaper never tired. It was his experience that the Medical Corps rarely came within rifle-range, and kept usually behind the field-artillery and battalion-headquarters. Always he had seen the battalion stretcher-bearers taking all the hardest kicks and receiving none of the ha'pence.

This was the more ungrateful from a man awaiting aid from the very men he was disparaging, but he was far too tired to be just. At last they were carrying him slowly down the road, stumbling often in the torn pavé, and continually dazed and dazzled by the thud and flash of the guns. Everitt saw that the eastern sky was flushing from grey to lilac and rose-red in the dawn. The new day revealed in an uncanny twilight the wreckage of a shattered country-side.

After half an hour's journey along the road, they turned aside into a muddy track cut through the wayside bank. This sloped downwards into a kind of cave between walls lined with muddy sandbags. The roof was made of an arched sheet of corrugated iron covered with more sandbags, and the whole daubed with mud as a screen from aeroplanes. The passage was exactly wide enough to admit a stretcher, but within it widened to a chamber perhaps twelve feet square. Soiled blankets formed the door, and light came from the white glare of an acetylene lamp hanging from a rafter. This was an advanced dressing-station – the first-aid house on the road to hospital. Round the walls stretchers were ranged on brackets, like berths in a cabin, and more stretchers covered every foot of the floor. Each carried its burden, muddy, bloody, hacked and mutilated sometimes almost beyond human resemblance. The place reeked of blood and mud and sweat and iodine: the air was foul with the stench of wounds. Some of the men were dead, some were dying, some were groaning, some were grinning, some were silent between clenched teeth. Beneath the lamps was a large trestle-table, and one by one the men were lifted upon it for examination by the doctors. As soon as this was completed, the stretcher was removed and carried out by a door opposite, and another entered to take its vacant place on the shelves: thus there was an unending stream of patients, in at one door and out at the other. It was salutary to remember that this stream had been flowing without respite now for days and weeks, and that it would continue to flow until the coming of the winter's lull. Everitt's turn came in half an hour, and he found himself recumbent beneath the glare of the lamp. Someone held to his lips an invalid's feeding-cup containing tea, hot, strong and sweet, and, rising upon the support of one arm, he drank noisily and greedily through the spout of the cup.

91

There were two doctors and perhaps half a dozen orderlies. One of them told Everitt they had been working there for twenty hours and must carry on until relief came. In that dazzling light their faces were white and ghastly, their eyes puffy for want of sleep, and all their movements languid with fatigue. (Everitt suddenly wondered what sort of scarecrow *he* must appear.) That unending stream of men had to be attended to somehow, patched up and forwarded to the clearing-station. And this was one dressing-station among hundreds – a drop in the ocean of suffering!

To Everitt's relief his leg was dismissed without examination. Evidently the field-dressing was adequate. His arm, however, they washed and dressed, slitting the sleeve of his tunic the better to reach the wound, and hurting him hideously where the linen beneath had stuck to the raw flesh. But the ordeal was soon over, and he found himself outside again and carried some fifty yards farther down the road. Near by dead men were being lifted from stretchers required urgently for more profitable burdens.

For a time he was left with some dozen others in the shelter of a stack of ammunition-cases. It was now broad day, and with the light came cheerfulness. The little group fell to an interminable discussion of the chances of Blighty, and swapped yarns blended of horror and humour. A stray shell, pitching perhaps twenty yards away, sobered them considerably, but in less than an hour appeared the eagerly expected ambulance. This, since the road was too rough for motors, was a clumsy, high-built wagon, canvas covered and daubed conspicuously with a soiled red cross. Two horses seemed fully as nervous as the driver.

The stretchers were run into their places, three ranged one above another on either side of a central gangway, and the straps tied to prevent their jerking from the grooves on the brackets. Everitt noticed one man particularly. He was swathed from head to middle in fold upon fold of bandages, already flushing to ominous red. With face dead-white, eyes tightly closed, and lips writhed apart to show clenched teeth, he had the appearance of a hideous Egyptian mummy, brutally ravished from a sepulchre.

The journey was an affair of half an hour only. Thanks to the torn roadway, the wagon rolled and jolted continually, and the wonder was that no one was thrown out. Everitt found it best to grip a stanchion with his sound arm and to project his injured leg over the corridor to prevent its injury. The men with body wounds suffered terribly from the shaking. Their groans were pitiable, but there was only the driver to hear them, and his attention was completely devoted to saving the horses from falling. A flapping canvas curtain hid the road, but an occasional glimpse showed that they were following the old route through Guillemont. No doubt they passed the Loamshires, but of them Everitt saw nothing.

Gradually they left the roar of guns behind them, and at last the ambulance stopped at a cross-road, where the passengers were unloaded into a field largely devoted to picketed mules. It seemed that the motor-ambulances ran from here rearwards, and already there was some fifty stretchers awaiting removal. They were back in the old 'line behind the line,' an ugly region of dumps and stores, horse-lines and light-railways, huts and tents and tangled telegraph wires. Traffic of lorries and ambulances covered the road, muddy indeed, but at least unbroken. The country crawled with troops coming and going. Everitt noticed that shrapnel helmets were no longer in use and cast away his own as a contribution to the local salvage-dump. Another link broken!

For an hour they lay there in the hot sunshine. Near by, a man shot through the lung tossed and tumbled in hopeless search of ease, and could find no one to help him. A few wandering samaritans administered water and cigarettes, and exchanged with them arid speculations on the 'duration.' High in the sky an aeroplane was surrounded with innumerable puffs of white cotton-wool, and near at hand an asthmatic anti-aircraft gun coughed with vicious impotence. In Everitt's ears the rush and hiss of shells still sounded continually. Sometimes he could hardly persuade himself that the sound was pure

94

imagination, and the sudden rush of escaping steam from an engine near by sent him cowering in an agony of dread. It was twenty-four hours before the shells ceased rushing through his brain.

But the bustle of the motor-ambulances revived him. By this time he was used to being treated like a parcel, and excitement grew with every stage of the journey. Naturally he was separated from his companions on the horse-ambulance, and indeed throughout the day he was continually cheek by jowl with strangers. Over firmer ground the going was easier, but on open stretches of road the greater speed of the car made the jolting as severe as ever. Sometimes they were delayed by traffic, and, raising the rear curtain, it was possible to look out upon the scarred wilderness beside the road, and the variegated multitude upon it. For some distance they were followed by the limbers of a battery of howitzers, and the gunners were quick with sympathy. Water and cigarettes were all they had to give, but they gave generously.

Everitt noticed that the gunners seemed impressed with the contents of the ambulance. Wholeheartedly they cursed the war, and, driven apparently by present evidence to a rare concession, even admitted that 'the infantry had the worst time of it.' For this is a sore point and an unending debate. The infantryman is doubtless prejudiced but, after all, he alone has the privilege of seeing each and every phase of active service, and can thus best judge the relative trials of the gunners, engineers, transport, and ambulances. The flying-corps (or that inconsiderable part of it that flies) is alone outside his ken, and for the rest, at one time or another, he shares the work of all. On the other hand none but himself know the full-fledged joys of the front of the front. Grotesquely enough, Everitt plumed himself complacently on his membership of the 'P.B.I.,' and, in face of this astounding confession, now felt more than ever competent to look down upon every other branch of the service. It is the same with every foot-slogger. He will curse his job wholeheartedly – 'all the work, most of the danger, and none of the trimmings,' but he never fails to remind all and sundry that the infantry, and the infantry alone, is winning (or losing) the war.

As they travelled along the crowded roads, Everitt hugged the thought that all these toiling hundreds were envying the men in the ambulances. Certainly he had always looked upon the wounded as lucky devils, and slowly he was becoming aware of his amazing good fortune. For some of the men in that particular ambulance the good fortune was not so obvious, but, despite his horrified sympathy for them, he could not repress an egotistical gloating over the unfortunates left to carry on. 'Damn you, Jack, I'm all right' is the Army's creed, and yet this callousness is inextricably mixed with the noblest self-sacrifice and a hundred odds and ends of altruism.

In less than an hour they reached a camp of large marquees, much like an old-time circus in appearance, lying close to the road, and on the site of the old front line. Beyond the tents a line of battered poplars only partly hid the roofs of a village, sadly enough ruined, but at least still recognizable. Here the Somme desert came abruptly to an end, and here grass was growing over the wounds of war. A large Red Cross flag waved over the marquees, and denoted the 'Collecting-Station' for the area. Once again the stretchers were unloaded, and the green canvas of a low-pitched marquee gave welcome shelter from a sun now hot enough for discomfort. Everitt found himself ranged on the earth floor on one side of a long range of inter-communicating pavilions. Once more he suffered qualms lest some enthusiast should experiment upon his leg, and again the air was charged with the odour of iodine and lysol.

In a little while he was placed upon a table for examination, and the dressing upon his leg replaced by a thick wad of bandages wound puttee-wise. A sketchy attempt to wash the wounds was exquisitely painful, and Everitt noticed that their hue had changed ominously to dark mulberry colour. Some one told him dispassionately that he was 'for the needle,' and before he had had time to speculate upon this terrifying announcement, an officer jabbed a hypodermic syringe into his right arm, squirted a measured quantity of serum into the wound,

97

and marked his wrist with a large 'T' in indelible
pencil. This 'T,' being interpreted, signified Anti-
Tetanus Injection – an inoculation against lock-
jaw, to which dirty wounds are normally susceptible.
Undoubtedly the treatment is efficacious, since
lockjaw was almost unknown in France, while in
other campaigns it has slain more men than battles.
Everitt was soon to grow used to the formality,
but on this first occasion he was amateurishly
interested.

Immediately afterwards he submitted to the
ordeal of the question – that wearisome catalogue
of particulars taken and retaken henceforwards at
every stage of the journey. Also he was provided
with a Field Casualty Card, whereon were scribbled
all possible particulars of his name, rank, regiment,
number, age, religion, length of service, and (all
that really mattered) the nature of his injury. With
a particularly silly thrill of pride – for the rôle of
living target is far from Homeric – he saw himself
grandiloquently described as a 'battle casualty.'
Decidedly the pride of the latter stages of casualty-
hood was a balm to the indignity of the earlier
proceedings. A doctor glanced at the card and
scrawled upon it something illegible which an
orderly said was 'evacuation.' The blessed word was
a passport to the Base, and incidently precluded
interference until he should reach that haven. For
fear of pain had now taken the place of fear of danger,
and Everitt was discovering that safety did not

after all fill full his cup of desire. The Base was now
his Mecca, and he felt utterly incapable of rest until
he reached it. And already it was plain that on
arrival there, Blighty in turn would usurp its place
as the true Island of the Blessed.

And so out into another tent, where tea and
bread and butter (marvellously cut into slices) made
what seemed a glorious meal. It was the first food
he had tasted in comfort since leaving Meaulte.
Then out to another fleet of ambulances, and away
to the Casualty Clearing-Station!

This second journey was longer, and soon all
traces of war's wreckage were left behind. The
houses were no longer ruined, nor the trees lopped
and shattered, nor the fields ploughed naked by the
shells. This was the normal world again, a smiling
country-side, ordinary enough in ordinary times,
but now by contrast seemingly the fairest land
beneath the sun. Not that evidence of the furnace
was wanting. Camps and dumps encroached upon
the fields, and all the roads were crowded with
lorries, but these things now seemed excrescences
upon the natural beauty of the landscape. A mile
or so away they were rather an essential part of
another dispensation.

It was little enough that Everitt saw of this, for
the warmth of the day made him glad to lie flat
upon his back in vacant contemplation of the roof
a foot above his eyes. The travelling was easier
over improving roads, and a cushion beneath his

knee gave him ease at last. The convoy turned off the road into a zone of tents, large enough almost to make an independent town. He was carried into a large marquee, perhaps a hundred feet long and fifty feet wide, filled everywhere, save for narrow gangways, with stretchers mounted on low trestles. This gave them the appearance of beds, and marked another stage towards civilization. Here too were Sisters in grey uniforms and crimson capes, cheering every one by their very presence, and calling all and sundry 'sonny.'

Almost the first words one of them spoke to Everitt were that if he felt able to write she would let him have a field-card or even a blank post card. To use the former he knew would raise a tempest of fear and doubt at home, for the bald statement, 'I am wounded,' may mean anything. Scribbling with the stump of a pencil, he achieved the following barbarous letter:

'DEAR MOTHER, —

'I have caught it in the leg, and am now in a field-hospital en route for the Base. I will write soon. DO NOT WORRY.'

— this last imbecility in capital letters. It was vilely crude, but in such circumstances there was little else to say. The censor would delete ruthlessly any hint of locality, and no one wishes to rhapsodize on a cruelly public post card. At the same time he was given a gaudy linen bag in which to store his belongings for safe transit. After the abandonments of the past two days these consisted of a jack-knife, a letter-case and letters, a Bible, a purse containing 7 francs and 50 centimes, a pocket edition of Omar Khay-yâm, a filthy khaki handkerchief, and an identity disc on a greasy piece of string round his neck. The Casualty Card remained tied to his tunic as a kind of Open Sesame.

No sooner was Everitt settled in his place than he was hailed by a neighbour. 'Why, Tom!' 'Hullo, Jack, what are you doing here?' 'Oh, same as you!' It was Jack Munro, of his old training platoon in England. They had slept as neighbours for six months at Salisbury, piled their bedding as a pair, grumbled in the same section, and marched in the same four. Munro was Scotch, dour, more than a little morose, and yet strangely given to spasmodic freaks of practical joking. (As when he upset every bed in the hut an hour after midnight.) Pawky and solemn and slow, it was rarely that he saw a joke, but when he did his sudden explosive guffaw frightened strangers. They had shared their parcels (one Kershaw making a third – their sec-tion-commander, promoted lance-corporal and long since returned to the Base with a weak heart), and it is remarkable that they had never quarrelled. They had been separated on joining the Tenth Loamshires overseas, and had since seen little of each other. And now they were thrown side by side by Fate and the Prussians.

For an hour there was no lack of talk between them. They compared notes of their experiences — they were both hit in the leg — and speculated wistfully on the future. Munro had got to know Everitt well enough to confide in him his love for the dearest girl in the world. Hardly a day passed (in England, at all events) when he neither wrote nor received a letter, and even her photograph had been dragged from its hiding-place. And when a Scotsman shows you his lassie's picture you may say you know him well. He was full of the prospect of seeing her soon, and told Everitt they were only awaiting the arrival of a train to be evacuated immediately to the Base. They plotted to ask the orderlies to place them in the same ward on the train, and even hoped to reach the same hospital.

The magic news of 'train up' followed hard upon a second meal. A fever of impatience possessed them when the first man was carried out — would the train be full before their turn came? The Sister's encouragement failed entirely to pacify them, and more than once Everitt felt like crawling to the train. At last they were carried to the door, and the stretcher placed upon frames mounted on wheels. Four stretchers, two above and two below, made a kind of coach, and orderlies pushed this along rails to the dark green ambulance-train that was waiting not a hundred yards away.

The light railway ran close beside the train, and Everitt and Munro grinned cheerfully on the journey. There was a spice of the Scenic Railway about it, and, to add to their sense of holiday, Everitt recognized the place as that same clearing-station they had seen packed with ominous crowds of wounded on their journey southwards.

As the men were lifting him from the train, Everitt caught sudden sight of Myers, in a snow-white head-bandage after the manner of an Arab sheikh, walking slowly towards the train not a dozen yards ahead. There was only time for a hurried shout: 'Good luck, old chap — you managed it, then,' and Myers, in his astonishment, could only grin hideously beneath his linen casque. Yet, even as he spoke, Everitt remembered guiltily his petulance of yesterday, and his almost incredible bad temper. What must Myers have thought of him? But there was no time now for talk, and their conversation was unavoidably delayed for six months. Munro, too, had disappeared into the train, and Everitt found himself separated from both friends at the same moment. They had not even time to say good-bye, and Everitt never saw him again. In England they maintained a strenuous correspondence, but by the time Everitt had rejoined his reserve battalion, Munro was in France a second time. The day after he rejoined the Loamshires he went over the top with the others and was killed outright. Just bad luck — a day's delay, and he would certainly have missed the attack! And the best girl in the world? History is silent, and in any case, what is one sorrow among millions?

V

ENTRAINING was a complicated business. The
rolling-stock was French, and consisted of con-
verted corridor-passenger coaches. Thus there were
none of the double sliding-doors of a genuine ambulance-train, and it was necessary to lift the stretcher
through the narrow doorways at the ends of the
coaches, and then sideways round sharp corners to
the compartment within. Further, there was no
platform or staging available, and the two foot-
boards of the train gave only a precarious foothold
to the bearers. The complicated manœuvre of load-
ing was only accomplished slowly and with difficulty. Half a dozen people seemed concerned with
each transhipment, and the luckless stretcher rocked
and swayed like a boat in storm. Everitt as nearly
as possible fell out bodily, and only saved himself
by clinging to whatever knobs and handles came
within his reach. At last, the stretcher having been
slued round into the carriage, it only remained to
hoist the occupant into his allotted berth.

The partitions of the compartments had been
removed, and each coach was divided into two
sections. On either side of a central corridor the
berths were arranged longitudinally in three tiers —
six berths to a section. To Everitt was assigned a
place on the top row, two feet from the roof. The
bearers raised the stretcher on their shoulders to an
elevation that was even then far from adequate.

Amid a chorus of guidance and encouragement he grasped straps hanging from the roof and hauled himself upwards and sideways into the berth above. The empty stretcher receded downwards to what seemed an immense distance.

The berth was a broad canvas hammock slung on frames, but, after the sharp discomfort of a succession of stretchers, it seemed a couch for a prince. There was a pillow, and four thick blankets, two above and two below, and the folds of these last successfully smothered the angularities of the frames. From this high perch Everitt could see that the other berths, to judge from groans and restless tossings, were occupied by serious cases: naturally the lighter casualties were stowed near the roof. Behind him a door gave admittance to some kind of store-room for dressings and utensils, and in front was the narrow pass by which he had entered. He lay so close to the roof that the windows were beneath him, but across the corridor he could glance downwards to the busy tramway.

He did not know how long it would take to load the train, and no one seemed able to enlighten him. By this time it was four o'clock, and the hot afternoon sun made the carriage intolerably stuffy. Everitt began to believe the journey might prove less amusing than he had been given to understand. There was nothing whatever to do, and he could only watch the movements outside at the expense of a crick in the neck. The man on the top berth opposite was too badly hurt to give any answer to his attempt at conversation, and Everitt in his loneliness discovered that he was incredibly tired and sleepy. An orderly approaching, he learned that the train was now fully loaded. 'But she never starts before midnight – else the Jerries 'ud see us, and there'd be dirty work.' Whether from guns or bombs he did not say, but the prospect of eight hours' delay was sufficiently depressing. Something of this must have appeared in his face, for the other was impelled to cheer him. 'Tea's at five and you'll be at Rouen to-morrow morning.'

This was news indeed. Rouen he had seen several times – a wide-spreading town standing finely in the broad Seine valley, noteworthy in passing for the steep wooded hills over the river, the grey Cathedral with its curiously truncated tower, and the iron suspension-bridge that carries the railway. He would rather it had been Abbeville or Boulogne, whence Blighty was obviously more accessible, but were there not ambulance-ships sailing direct from Rouen riverwards to Southampton? The orderly confirmed this, and, learning the extent of Everitt's hurts, told him he was 'a dead cert for Blighty.' 'They're bunged up with bad cases at all the Bases – too bad to move – and they daren't keep any others there long.'

This was better still and a third meal went far to bind the spell – hot tea in enamelled bowls (blue outside and white within), bread and butter spread with liberal jam, and actually a hunk of cheese to follow. The friendly orderly – a pale, weedy, spectacled youth in baggy trousers – brought him another pillow to ease his injured leg, and in something very like contentment Everitt pulled the blankets over his head to chew the cud of comfort.

For to be in repose of mind and body after long weeks of suffering is perhaps the greatest blessing the weary world can show. He must have seemed an object pitiable enough, soiled with dirt and sweat, ragged and unshaven, but to lie there in comfort, free for the time from pain, secure from danger, exulting in the knowledge that in a few hours he would be carried away from all the complicated horrors of war, was a very fair substitute for Heaven.

In a few minutes he must have been asleep, for, opening his eyes again, he found that night had fallen. The train was motionless, but he had no notion if it were still in the clearing-station. The compartment, dimly lit by a shaded lamp round which moths were dancing feverishly, was eerie enough in the gloom. Occasionally a groan or a curse came from a man suffering beyond endurance. The air was rank with exhalations, hot, stuffy, and intolerably offensive. Dirt, stale sweat, dried blood, varnish and a smell of drugs and food contended together in a sickening medley. Outside the guns still boomed in harsh chorus, softened by distance from a bark to a roar, but tireless as ever. Someone said it was ten o'clock and consigned the Red Cross to Hell for the delay.

A little later came the Doctor and Sister on their rounds. In that crowded box there was little they could do – largely their duty was to change essential dressings, make minor adjustments for comfort's sake, and, principally and above all, to speak a cheering word to souls sorely in need of it. Always the men tried to catch the Sister's eye, eager for a word, and grinning with gratification when they received it. Once again they were all 'sonny,' and it was not only the five 'Woodbines' that made them glad to see her. With their departure Everitt dozed and waked and dozed again. At last a jerk told him that the train had started, and that Jerry had once again been cheated.

The night's journey was a nightmare. At the time Everitt was perhaps too tired to think about what he saw, just as, in the line, the need for violent action between bouts of bemused exhaustion had drugged his brain to numbness. But afterwards every detail grew vivid to memory. At home in England he would go over the whole journey again from Les Bœufs to Rouen, visualizing every detail, trembling and growing sick with horror at these vivid night-thoughts, shaking with panic to think of dangers that were passed.

The train took thirty hours to reach Rouen –

from midnight on Tuesday to the early hours of
Thursday morning, and they had been eight hours
in their cots before it started. Everitt passed the
time in broken dozes, which at first seemed to
refresh him, but afterwards served only to exas-
perate him by their brevity. Several times during
the night a doctor or a Sister visited them, asked
in a whisper if all were well, and passed on noise-
lessly. Some of the men near him were desperately
injured. The tattered thing in the cot opposite on
the lowest tier was bandaged from neck to waist,
and lay there hour after hour groaning through set
teeth, too ill to move so much as a finger. Only the
most desperately urgent operations could be attempted in a moving train, and all they could do
for him was to inject morphia and sponge his face
and lips. Another man was mangled so ruthlessly
with shrapnel in the back and buttocks that he
could find no position of comfort. Howsoever he
tossed and shifted, he could not relieve the pressure
on the wounds — great raw surfaces as though he
had been flayed.

All the night long the orderlies were busy bringing draughts of water to burning throats, changing
bandages when necessary, talking to those whom
pain made garrulous. The grotesque horrors of the
night made Everitt sick to see; the Sisters and
orderlies performed for helpless men the vilest
offices. And always the train was rumbling
through the darkness, while the cots swayed and

rocked, and men grew light-headed with pain and fever.

As far as Amiens the line was blocked with every kind of traffic – fodder for the Push in the shape of men, horses, guns and stores. On their journey southwards Everitt had been astonished by the volume of the traffic behind the rail-heads, and had counted the ambulance-trains with something like personal dismay. Thus the present delay was readily explicable.

The grey morning found them still jogging towards the north-west. The day was passed principally in waiting for meals. The kitchen, for convenience' sake in respect of water, lay immediately behind the engine, and the orderlies must utilize the frequent halts for the carrying of the pails of tea and porridge and trays of bread and bacon along the track from coach to coach. Thus much of the food was cold by the time it reached its destination.

There were no platforms between the coaches, and doctors and Sisters alike swung themselves from one to another by means of the stanchions beside the doors. Only thus had they been able to follow their night-rounds. Everitt, of course, had seen nothing of this, and now only learned it from the friendly orderly together with other vivid details of what he called a dog's life. The gymnastics involved in rushing up and down the track beside the slowly moving train and in swinging the heavy pails to and from the coaches were alone almost enough to tire a man at the end of a day. Add to this the vile duties of the sick bays, and it was clear that even the Red Cross behind the line had its strenuous moments. Their rest, it seemed, came on the return journey to the clearing-station, but before they could 'get down to it,' it was necessary to scrub and scour every corner of the train and every article in it.

Dinner was an affair of stew and potatoes, bread and rice; tea copied yesterday. Between these sole breaks in the monotony Everitt dozed and exchanged jerky conversation with the man opposite. Also he hoarded scanty cigarette-ends, and once nearly fell headlong in trying to reach across the gangway for a match. Someone loaned him a magazine, bursting with War jokes, and crammed with optimism and robust cheer. But he found reading difficult, and dozed the more as the day grew warmer.

As the chill morning brightened towards noon he was perplexed to notice the air more and more strongly infected with a hideous carrion reek, such as was already only too familiar. The stench seemed more offensive whenever in his twistings and turnings he raised the folds of the blanket on his cot. The sickening sweetish odour filled him with a shuddering disgust, and appetite fled. The strangeness of the thing puzzled him, but it was only in Hospital at Rouen that he learned its meaning. Apologizing shamefacedly to an orderly there, the latter replied cheerfully: 'Not a bit of it. Of course she's bound to hum after all those hours in the train with never a dressing. They'll clean it out for you to-morrow in the butcher's shop, and you'll be as sweet as a bloody rose.' He realized that he had no cause to feel shamed like a detected leper. His wound had turned septic and that vile odour of decay was part of the day's work.

All that day the train jolted through the hot plain of Normandy, and the men grew languorous in the heat. In that polluted air the coolness of evening was doubly welcome, but it was not until ten o'clock on Wednesday night that they reached the sidings and ghastly flickering arc-lamps of Rouen. The delay there was exasperating. Six times they passed the illuminated face of a clock below a signal-cabin, each time on a different pair of rails. Complicated manœuvres of shunting followed, and the train entered the station three times before reaching its destination.

Excitement now kept every one awake, and rumour declared that a boat was waiting at the quay to ship the whole trainload to England. Jerked downwards and outwards on the stretcher, Everitt found himself on a long platform paved with wounded. The arc lamps showed the dimly lighted train disgorging streams of helpless and grotesquely bandaged men, the platform crowded with strange-looking figures arrayed in rags and tatters of muddy khaki and white linen, and a long line of Red Cross Ambulances filling rapidly and driving

away into the darkness. It was early morning
before Everitt found a place in one of them, and by
then nothing seemed to matter but a bed. There
were stories of spring-mattresses, sheets and feather
pillows, and filthy as any tramp though he knew
himself to be, he felt perfectly willing to crawl con-
tentedly into such a nest of bliss and sleep indefinitely.

At this hour of the morning the town was dark
and silent, and their destination uncertain: England
was obviously as remote as ever. The night air was
cool and refreshing; the flash and roar of the guns
were quenched at last. In half an hour they saw
lights beside the road and on a board the legend
'No. 1 General Hospital'; and there followed a long
succession of similar boards numbered consecu-
tively. The Hospital area covered many acres, but
in the gloom it was impossible to see anything save
the grey shapes of buildings.

At No. 5 board they swung away from the road
and halted before a brightly lit double doorway.
Here they were carried into a long bare waiting-
room already occupied by fifty stretchers. Following the inevitable Inquisition came the night-
Sister in the silent ward, clean, sweet-smelling
sheets, the discarding of the grimed rags of the
journey, and billow upon billow of slumber and
sweet forgetfulness.

Here was the Base at last, after a journey of thirty
hours from the rail-head, and sixty hours from

no-man's-land. For Everitt at least 'The Somme' was a memory.

But not far away the fires of hate burned red as ever, and the long agony quickened with the days.

THE COWARD

'He that outlives this day, and comes safe home,
Will stand a tip-toe when this day is nam'd,
And rouse him at the name of Crispian.'

KING HENRY V

I

WE two were alone in the carriage and entire strangers. The War-to-end-War was already a memory, and we were travelling together from London towards the West. Falling easily into talk after the garrulous manner of holiday-makers, we drifted from the time-honoured conventions of the weather gradually but surely towards the Great Tragedy. There followed the inevitable question – 'What were you in?' and we fell to discussing War in the abstract, the ethics of it, and the alternatives promised by the League of Nations.

My companion professed himself so rabid a Pacifist that I could not help asking him how it was he had ever worn khaki. He replied with unexpected fierceness that he had been bullied into soldiering, and had only joined the Army to avoid ridicule. He had always hated War, and realized the horror and folly of it; but better these things than the degradation of white feathers. For the same reason he had joined an Infantry battalion – 'so that they shouldn't mock me any longer.' It seemed that his subsequent adventures had served merely to confirm his prejudices.

The talk turned to cowardice, and to what extent it is a crime in War. I noticed that my companion was growing strangely excited, and, on my remarking that a deserter could expect no mercy, he cried out at me that it was a pity that those who framed

119

such harsh judgments could not themselves be put to the test. Experience would probably broaden their charity.

Seeing myself to be treading on dangerous ground I hastened to admit with due humility that I had spoken without knowledge. A civilian had obviously no experience of these things. He seemed mollified by my apology, and asked me if I cared to hear a story. Scenting a yarn of the War, I laid aside my newspapers, and he needed no further encouragement.

II

WHEN the Germans made their big Push in the spring of 1918, we were on the right flank of the British line, leading a gipsy life in the forest country between Noyon and Laon. Immediately in front of us lay La Fère, hidden in the woods of St. Gobain, and our own position was that of support-battalion in the Bois de Coucy, just south of the Oise River. I say that this was our position, but in point of fact I knew little about it. For more than a fort-night, thanks to the prosaic infliction of a sore leg, I had been resting in a field-hospital.

On the 20th March the ambulance brought me back to the horse-lines, three or four kilometres behind no-man's-land. My feet had barely touched ground when the old familiar atmosphere of surmise and vague suspicion closed round me like a fog. For weeks, you will remember, the Allies in the west had been kept on the knife-edge of suspense. When would the Germans launch their offensive? When and where? No one knew, but the humblest private had his theory, and the nearer you were to the line the wilder and more circumstantial grew the rumours. Even before my holiday we had more than once been the victims of a premature alarm. 'Jerry' was coming over to-day, or to-night, or to-morrow at dawn. Orders and counter-orders circulated dizzily, elaborate preparations were made and can-celled; the waiting and uncertainty keyed men's nerves to an intense pitch of apprehension; and always nothing happened.

The Fifth Army had recently taken over a wide sector from the French, and, as is now well known, the available troops were insufficient to hold it. The system of defences in a notoriously quiet region had been long neglected, and were now entirely inadequate. Foch's strategic Reserve (for even thus early we called it his) was doubtless ready and waiting to go wherever it might be called, but local supports of our own were an unknown quantity.

Since the 6th February the battalion had been out of the line only four days, and these were spent in moving from one place to another. Moreover, be the line never so quiet, the life in cramped and stuffy dug-outs, the long days passed in patrol work and sentry duty, the makeshift rations, the lack of baths and clean clothes – all these things tell on men's nerves and weaken their stamina. Over and above these normal troubles was the sense of great and terrible events in preparation, of a storm soon to burst no one knew where. On our front the Germans were quiet enough (too quiet according to the experts), but we spared no efforts to strengthen our defences. Night and day we dug new trenches, and wired and camouflaged them feverishly. At other times we carried strange burdens from the transport lines to the trenches, where, thanks to hard work, we slept like logs and fed like famished savages. And each day we 'stood-to' in the frosty

dawn for an attack that was always postponed to
to-morrow.

For myself, I was a disconsolate schoolboy at the
end of his holiday, and, the spell of routine broken,
I came back to the line perhaps stronger in body,
but in spirit more than ever unwilling. Almost at
once I learned that I had returned at an unlucky
moment. As I left the Chauny highway for the road
that climbs the hill to Sinceny, a divisional-signaller
told me that all troops were 'standing-to' and that
stragglers had been recalled to quarters. After the
freedom from toil and worry that makes the roughest
field-ambulance so desirable a refuge, this news sent
my spirits to zero. The mouse was safely in the trap
again, and this time the cat was waiting for him.
For a solitary journey such as mine breaks a man's
courage; it is only when he is alone that such sickly
imaginings have him at their mercy. Among his
chums he has other things to think of.

Our Reserve Company was billeted in huts by the
wayside and the men were standing to arms, ready
to march. Dispatch-riders raised clouds of dust on
the road, and a Brigadier passed in his car like
a pale image of evil tidings. A sergeant-major,
with a great show of unconcern, gave me his opinion
that the whole thing was 'pure wind up.' Brigade
Headquarters was near at hand, however, and there
I sought out a friend whose duties in the canteen
brought him into close touch with the Mighty. But
although attaching superstitious importance to any

news from so exalted a quarter, I could learn little from him. Certainly an attack was expected; it might materialize or it might not. That was the sum of his knowledge; but I could see from the anxious faces of the satellites that hover ever in the shadow of the Staff that this time something was going to happen.

Nothing out of the way marked my journey to the line. Sinceny village had been smashed and gutted from end to end – deliberate damage effected by the Germans in their retreat to the Hindenburg Line a year ago. An empty doll's carriage stood crazily upon a heap of broken bricks. The gaudy wirework decorations in the tombs in the churchyard were broken and strewn upon the ground. The gravestones themselves were torn and shattered.

The usual rumours were afloat at Battalion Headquarters, and I heard that after this present spell in the line the Division was going to Italy, Egypt and Salonica. Like many another unit, we were always on the point of departure for the Antipodes, but a perverse destiny never allowed us to start. We discussed the possibilities of leave, and decided that recent declarations in Parliament could not but improve matters. As to the enemy's offensive, perhaps it would never come; and if it did, it would fail and be a thing of the past long before midsummer. It would be his last effort and, once we had weathered it, the end could not be much longer delayed. The coming of a group of R.A.M.C. men, detached from a field-ambulance for special service, sobered us a little, but we had heard the cry of 'Wolf' too often and laughed at their fears. Within a week the joke was a sour one.

Headquarters lay in dug-outs beneath twin hills known as the Buttes de Rouy, and the road threaded the valley between them to the village of Amigny-Rouy, where I hoped to find my Company. At dusk I followed the ration-carts through the deserted village, smashed like Pompeii of old, smashed in cold blood by bomb and mine and fire. The bright moonlight could not lighten the sombre sadness of its desolation, and memories and regrets lurked sadly among the shadows. Each house was a mangled skeleton – the windows blown out, the walls for the most part ruinous. In several places an interior lay exposed in section like a builder's plan, the intimacies of wall-paper and furniture clinging crazily to the tottering walls. Piles of rubble surrounded these grotesque ruins, and only the main road had been cleared for traffic.

It was a still and peaceful evening. Not a gun was firing, and the crack of a sniper's rifle or the quick chatter of machine-guns broke rarely through the silence. Woodland odours scented the air and, away from the shattered husk of the village, the smirch of War could easily be forgotten. But as dusk grew to dark, bright Verey lights soared high above the trees, climbed and hovered and fell, and changed the dark forest into fairyland.

125

My platoon I found in one of half a dozen inter-communicating dug-outs, dark narrow caverns, buried thirty feet below ground and, unless shell-fire blocked the entrances, safe from everything but gas. My return was hailed as a miracle of ill-fortune, for up here in the line every one seemed resigned to the worst. Letters and rations distributed, we exchanged contradictory rumours, and tried to draw comfort from a local theory that no German attack could by any possibility reach us through the thickly-wired forest.

The dug-out was lined on either side with a double tier of wire cots, like bunks in a ship's cabin. Each cot afforded its owner just room enough to lie curled up like a cat. Close to his hand were rifle, helmet, and gas-mask. His equipment lay at his feet, and his pillow was a greasy knapsack; ground-sheet and leather jerkin softened the scanty straw; his body he rolled in a muddy blanket.

Rations for to-morrow were stored in mess-tin and haversack, where bread and cheese and raisins, butter and bully-beef, socks and soap and chocolate, mingled affectionately together.

A candle-end, welded by its own grease to the timber-work of the dug-out, gave a smoky, flickering light: a careless elbow now and again jerked it head-long into the straw.

That night the narrow cots held some thirty men, who were unable to sit upright unless they swung their legs over the edge of their bed and crooked their necks to avoid the rough wire and timber. Some were brewing tea in mess-tins over ingenious portable cookers (made from cans of rifle-oil, with strips of 'four by two' for wick, or from rags floating in a tin of melted dubbin). Others were eating their supper, killing lice, cleaning rifles, writing letters, playing noisily at cards, reading, quarrelling, shaving and sleeping. So long as they were awake they were all busy. Meditation was unpopular.

Early in the evening the growl of guns had broken out northwards towards St. Quentin, but now all was quiet again. It was intense drum-fire while it lasted, however, and might well carry a definite warning. We drank the rum-ration, an all too scanty mouthful (the sergeants knew why); we blew out the lights; save for the whisper of the sentries by the brazier in the doorway, all was quiet in the dug-out. 'Get as much rest as you can, boys, for you may have a busy day to-morrow.'

III

WE were aroused by the grumbling thunder of guns. For a few minutes those who were first awake lay half-conscious of the sound and wondering idly what it might mean: then came remembrance and with it fear. Lights gleamed here and there in the gloom and men rose in their cots and asked one another what was the matter. They knew only too well, but it comforted them to ask. In a few minutes someone went outside to see how things were going, but almost immediately he returned in company with the gas-guards nominally on duty. As they blundered down the stairs one man caught his finger in his trigger, and fired mercifully into the floor. The noise and the acrid smell of the explosion thoroughly aroused us. There was no longer any doubt; the long-threatened day had dawned at last.

The noise of the gun-fire was deadened by the long double flight of stairs and the two heavy gas-curtains made of Army blankets, but the sentries reported that a heavy barrage was falling some hundred yards behind the line of the dug-outs. That there was danger was evident from their haggard faces and nervous, jerky movements. Obviously they had stood at their posts until lonely men could endure no longer.

The attack could not come before dawn, and we thus had before us at least three hours of nerve-racking idleness. Would they man battle positions now, or wait for daylight? Suspense and ignorance were maddening, and, feeling I could remain quiet no longer, I determined to venture above ground.

In a moment I left behind me the warmth and light of the dug-out, the comforting presence of my fellow-prisoners, and the sound and solace of their voices. The dull growl and rumble outside grew abruptly louder and more menacing. In the dense darkness of the stairs I groped my way slowly from landing to landing, finding the gas-curtains by blundering into them, and tripping over the weighted blocks that held them down. At the mouth of the shelter the night was as dark as the pit. Behind the German lines thousands of guns were in action, the sound of their firing like water bubbling in a cistern – like, but infinitely louder. From the east there rushed a steady, never-ceasing stream of shells, the clamour of their onset rising to a menacing climax overhead. Despite their hideous roar and racket, they gave me the impression that they were in no sort of hurry, but intended to persevere in their remorseless task of destruction until all resistance had been smashed to dust and ashes. A little way ahead, among the shattered houses and orchards of Amigny, they were bursting with a ringing, rending crash, magnified, if that were possible, by the echo from the walls. The glare of explosions stained the night like lightning. Everywhere I could hear the whizz and ping of scattering fragments.

The danger was real enough, though the darkness

and the early hour exaggerated it, and it was with a sinking heart that I stumbled downstairs again to the perplexed Council of War among the shadows. And there we remained for several hours, wondering and conjecturing and prophesying. It seemed clear enough that we were cut off from our supports by the bombardment, but we had no means of discovering what was happening elsewhere. We were a little group of shipwrecked adventurers, isolated from the world, boxed up in a cave, and liable to instant death or mutilation if we left our shelter. For that is the danger of dug-outs – they sap the morale of those who use them. It is safe down there, and the temptation is to stay down indefinitely until the enemy appears at the entrance with bomb and rifle.

The gun-fire was growing heavier, and crashing blows drove home apparently just overhead. Deadened though they were by the thickness of earth, yet the ground shook, the candles shuddered, and a dull concussion blunted our senses. Sometimes two or three buffets fell in quick succession on the roof. What must be the turmoil outside when such an effect could be felt thirty feet below ground? Suppose a shell blocked the stairways! It is another disadvantage of thus hiding in safety that dismal forebodings darken a mind that has no necessary work to distract it. I imagined a feverish digging for life, while the air grew slowly fouler and strength failed relentlessly.

It was essential that someone should take over the gas-guard, but the service was not a popular one. The sentry must stand in the open and, from the scanty shelter of a wooden sentry-box, be ready to sound the alarm on a wooden rattle or an empty shell-case used bell-fashion. Even short spells of half an hour thus employed seemed an eternity, and the relief men sometimes sought to escape duty by pretending to doze in their bunks. The danger was invested with the horror of the unknown and imperfectly realized, and we tried in vain to extract grains of comfort from the sentries as they returned. 'How's things up above, chum? Is it light yet? Is he slacking off?' And always the same reply: 'Pretty thick, mate. Pretty thick.'

Once there came an alarm and the sweetish, cloying smell of 'pineapple gas.' We muzzled ourselves in our masks and sat for a time in a compulsory silence, like a legion of dumb and hideous devils, but the heat of the masks, the blindness caused by condensed moisture on the windows, the foul taste of the rubber mouthpieces, the choking pressure of the nose-clips – these various torments made us ready to take risks. Men were continually removing their masks in order to taste the air, and for the most part held them hanging from their cases.

Breakfast was an affair of bread and cheese and water, for the cook-house, a crazy shed of corrugated iron some hundred yards from shelter, was deserted and inaccessible. It was certain that this was the last

131

meal some of us would ever eat, but on the surface at all events we preserved a semblance of cheerfulness. Again and again we told one another that the attack, when it came (for we were so far resigned now), must needs break itself upon our elaborate preparations. Thus, above a current of fear and disgust we yet managed to build a bridge of hope, and we built it of various materials. Some were feverishly gay, and sang and laughed for all the world like men on a picnic. Others took refuge in a lighthearted cynicism, and assumed that the worst always happens and that nothing goes right beneath the sun – a useful pose beneath which Atkins habitually hides his deeper feelings. Others again remained impassive and resolutely unimpressed. My own feeling was of exasperation at being caught so narrowly in the trap. Spoiled by a fortnight's good living, and morbidly convinced that bad would go to worse, I had an uneasy consciousness of a tired battalion dispirited and exhausted by weeks of anxious forebodings.

The meal was too poor to cheer us after the manner of bacon and hot tea, and afterwards we had nothing to do but forecast the future. Some of the men, too excited to rest, took refuge in cards and argument, but the majority simply squatted in their bunks, waiting, and waiting, and waiting. Can you imagine that dark, gloomy, noxious cavern, lit dimly by guttering candles and ever and again shaken by the tremendous concussions overhead; the dirty, haggard faces asking dumbly why this horror had come upon them? They were waiting to be called into an inferno of iron and lead and choking gases, where dust and smoke and monstrous spouts of earth were writhing among shattered houses, and trees and hedges were splintering fast to matchwood. It is a damning admission, and one probably unique in the annals of War, but the spirit of the troops was not entirely excellent.

I V

At length our fears were realized, and the Captain of our Company roused us to man battle positions. Mr. Stewart was a tough, hard-bitten little Scotsman and, out since Mons, was by no means prone to panic; but then, if ever, I read in his face an ill-controlled foreboding. Scourged by his impatience, we seized rifles and equipment and stumbled clumsily towards the stairs. Dawn had broken outside, but a thick mist hid the sun. The Germans could have asked for nothing better. You could not see ten yards.

Once outside and hurrying towards the trenches, we lost that feeling of trapped helplesssness that made the dug-out so terrible a resting-place. The bombardment was now falling on the village some forty or fifty yards behind us, and Amigny was visibly falling to pieces. Clouds of dust and smoke, rose-coloured from the shattered brick-work, rose continually among the collapsing houses, and from these shifting volcanoes there rained bricks and timber and clods of earth and splintered trunks of trees. On the hard pavé of the roads the shells could make but little impression (although there they were the more dangerous by reason of flying fragments of stone), but elsewhere they dug smoking craters in the scorched and tumbled meadows.

Ducking our heads instinctively, we hurried towards a narrow fire-trench that opened from a lane

134

that four years ago was a leafy haunt of lovers. The shelter was meagre, but we entered it with an ostrich sigh of satisfaction. This was no consolidated line with revetted traverses and sand-bagged parapet, but merely a roughly dug and tortuous ditch, perhaps six feet deep and for the most part three feet wide. The crumbling fire-steps were growing muddy with the thaw of last night's frost. A hit anywhere near the brink of the trench would have smashed it in an instant, but by crouching frogwise below the parapet we found shelter from ground-shrapnel.

Distributing ourselves in groups of two and three along the trench, we mounted our Lewis guns with pans fully charged for firing, leaned cocked rifles with fixed swords against the parapet, and removed from bandoliers all surplus ammunition. And everybody lit a cigarette. It is well known that the consumption of cigarettes varies directly with the strength of the bombardment. To crouch in a hole, thinking of what may be about to happen — that way lies madness. Four cynics even made bold to defy Fate with a game of nap.

While we stood smoking, Captain Stewart and his batman appeared suddenly above the parapet. The latter was carrying a dozen S.O.S. rockets, which he distributed among us with the air of a man bestowing charity. Poor 'Minnie' West, so nicknamed by reason of a falsetto voice and a finicking manner, did not appear to enjoy his errand, ducked nervously at any nearer shell, and grinned only half-heartedly at sarcastic references to Guy Fawkes. Immediately to our right the trench-line turned backwards among the last houses of the village, and was accordingly exposed to the full strength of the barrage. The right flank of the Company was thus the post of greatest danger, and in a few minutes came the call for stretcher-bearers. Minnie had been unlucky. For that is the Army's formula of sympathy. A man has been blown to pieces, or detailed to peel potatoes, or drowned in a shell-hole, or robbed of his rations. His friends have only one comment to make: 'He's unlucky.' And after all, what more is there to say?

All the morning we remained idle in the trench. Whenever a shell fell short we ducked and dodged convulsively, aware of the futility of such action, but powerless to avoid it. Shell splinters flew past our heads and between our legs, and once a fragment of jagged steel whizzed viciously against the back of a man who was peacefully writing letters. For a moment we thought that he was wounded, but the crossed straps of his equipment had softened the blow, and beneath the half-severed leather there was nothing to see but a dull red bruise. Every one sympathized with him, and he resumed his letter in the spirit of a man with a grievance. To miss a 'Blighty One' is the great misfortune. Any moderate degree of maiming carries with it the certainty of rest and peace and cleanliness, and (who knows?) the possibility of the crowning mercy of a 'ticket.'

Somewhere about noon a shell knocked out an isolated Strong Point on our right flank, smashed the Lewis gun, and killed three of the gunners. Shortly afterwards another shell fell within a yard of the survivors as they were busily mounting another gun. This time no one was wounded, but the concussion stunned the Section-leader; and his chums, demoralized by misfortune, took matters into their own hands and abandoned their post. With them they dragged laboriously the unconscious corporal, blackened with stinking smoke, groaning feebly, and bleeding from nose and ears. In a little while, however, he had recovered, and they were once again mounting their gun in a new and safer position.

For this desertion they stood in little danger of a reprimand. Save for the Captain's visit just after our arrival we had so far seen only one officer – a subaltern who made one hurried tour of the trench and then vanished suddenly in the direction of Headquarters. And indeed at such times it is often no easy matter for Atkins to discover the whereabouts of those leaders he is universally reputed to adore. Normally, on these occasions the parade-martinets and inspectors of brass buttons are far too busy organizing victory in a dug-out to concern themselves with discipline, and thus the deserters need have no fear of either discovery or punishment.

Twelve hours had passed since our first arousing, and still there was no sign of an attack. Away to the north the roar of the bombardment seemed louder than ever, and mingled with it we could now hear the deadliest sound in warfare, the angry chatter of machine-guns. All the afternoon their staccato rattle continued. We guessed that a fierce attack was being pushed to desperation beyond the river, but no one knew with what success. I say no one knew, but towards evening the first definite rumours crept to us by way of runners from Battalion Headquarters. The Germans, so they said, had attacked over the whole front from Arras to La Fère, and had broken through a five-mile sector to a depth of three. There was also current a suspiciously circumstantial story that south of the river they would follow up a nine hours' high-explosive bombardment with four hours' gas shelling as a prelude to attack. We were in no mood to disbelieve the wildest tales and, cleaning and re-cleaning our rifles, argued and speculated continually. Long after noon, however, the big howitzer shells were still bursting in a steady stream. Four o'clock came and no gas alarm! It seemed probable we should see no Germans until to-morrow.

During the afternoon the cooks ventured to light fires in the open. They boiled water for tea, and even fried some war-worn bacon; and with this, our rations of bread and cheese, and a tin of sardines, we made what was almost a cheerful meal. 'The grub puts guts into you,' and we now felt twice the men to grapple with our troubles. In retrospect it seems amusing enough to pause midway in a mouthful of bread and bacon in order to estimate the changing range of the barrage. The ear automatically picks out from the roar of the bombardment the angry whirr of one shell nearer than others. Should the threat pass very closely, every one crouches as flat as may be among the sooty dixies, mingling gulped tea with lurid blasphemy. The noise of an express train grows in a swift crescendo, passes overhead with a vicious, deep-toned hum, and, changing suddenly to a fiercely-purposeful, downward-rushing whizz, culminates not twenty yards away in the shattering roar of an explosion that resembles nothing so much as the careless unloading of a cargo of iron rails. And so back to tea and bacon.

Towards evening the fog melted beneath a jovial sun that mocked men's madness from a cloudless sky. We could now see the flat fields ahead, covered with the rustling skeletons of last year's uncut hay, and the tortuous line of our wire half-way towards the forest. Danger of surprise being thus greatly lessened, some of the men were allowed to return to the dug-out for two hours' rest. Down in the gloom of the cave the noise of the guns slackened to a hoarse rumbling, and, free for the moment from the fear of pouncing danger, we could relax tired limbs in the straw and forget our troubles in an instant slumber. This two hours' shelter from the storm came to us like a reprieve to a condemned man. It seemed almost criminal to waste such precious

139

moments in sleep, but the majority could not have remained awake had their lives depended on it. They sank like logs into their cots, and, when roused again two hours later, grumbled venomously that they had not been resting for five minutes.

We stood-to in the half-light of dusk, and then waited in bright moonlight that presently faded to darkness lit by the gleam of guns. Towards midnight all save two men at each post were recalled to the dug-out; outside, the unlucky sleepy sentries watched patiently for dawn. And so ended for us one of the bloodiest days in the history of that blood-stained year. We had escaped the worst, and our casualties were few. But how were we to interpret those sinister rumours of events across the river?

V

THE two succeeding days we passed on a knife-edge of perplexity and apprehension. On the third evening we had official news from Corps Headquarters that the enemy had broken completely through the advanced posts and battle positions of the Fifth Army, and was thought to be within a few miles of Chauny. This was serious news indeed, for if he should enter the town and destroy the bridges over the Oise, we should be cut off by the river, not only from the remainder of the Division, but from the whole British Army. The lines of communication directly to our rear were used entirely by the French, and all our supplies came from the north-west. The forest extended to within little more than a mile of Chauny, and if this narrow gap were once closed, our only line of retreat must pass through the tangled thickets of the Bois de Coucy, where it would be impossible to maintain either coherence or discipline. No rumour was too wild to find backers. A French Army Corps was detraining behind us. (This I was afterwards able to confirm: it was part of Foch's Army of Manœuvre.) Five hundred men were besieged in Fort Vendeuil. The Guards had relieved the garrison there and swept the Germans back to the river.

In this welter of confusion and contradiction no one knew what to believe, and nerves and tempers alike were chafed to desperation. Anxiety played strange tricks with us. One man muttered to himself continually, gazing at the ground with strained, bloodshot eyes and answering not a word to question or entreaty. After a time his mutterings grew louder. 'Here's a bloody mess. Here's a bloody mess.' Again and again he repeated these words, and neither threats nor laughter could rouse him. So obstinate an introspection could have but one end, and at roll-call on the third day he did not answer his name. Fear had unhinged his mind. What became of him I never discovered.

Our days we spent in the trenches, sometimes asleep, but for the most part keeping our cover. The news gradually confirmed our fears. It became more and more certain that we were outflanked on our left, and to guard against this new danger we began digging trenches and Strong Points at right angles to the existing line Wire we had none, but we hid the newly turned earth under swathes of weeds and grasses and took advantage of hedges and trees for cover. The night we parcelled out between us so that two men shared guard for a couple of hours at each post. By the time ten men had completed their turns dusk had changed to dawn, and once again we stood-to in expectation of the crisis.

The barrage seemed to slacken slightly after the first twelve hours, but it may have been merely that we were growing accustomed to it. Communication with Headquarters was often interrupted, and the telephone more often than not useless. The signallers were thus constantly at work upon the ground-wires in search of a breakage, and no considerations of danger were allowed to hinder their almost continuous labours. Somehow the wires were repaired; somehow the ration-parties struggled through the barrage. These journeys were deservedly unpopular, but they were an essential service, and few escaped their varied excitements.

I was twice detailed for a fatigue-party to carry rations from 'B' Company in support to Platoon Headquarters. The whole length of tottering, battered Amigny lay between us and our objective, and it was out of the question to reach it by way of the main road. Accordingly our circuitous route took us through the scattered copses in front of our trench, and thence by a maze of lanes and footpaths round the right flank of the village. By this means we avoided the worst of the barrage, and, stumbling through the barriers of invisible barbed-wire that blocked the roads at every turning, ran, and walked, and ran again, to tumble breathlessly into shelter at the end of the journey.

Returning heavily-laden – for no one wished to make a double journey – we must needs walk slowly beneath our burdens. (I remember there fell to my share a sinister box of chloride of lime.) The weight of equipment and a slung rifle gnawed savagely at our shoulders. By journey's end we were dripping with sweat and panting like overdriven horses. Thirst sent caution to the winds, and, reckless of dysentery, we filled our bottles at the crazy well beside the cross-roads.

It was on the second night that we first heard the distinctive whistling and popping of gas-shells. These symbols of civilization, however, burst with but a feeble explosion (that the vapour might not be unduly dissipated), and accordingly lacked the moral effect of high explosives. On our ration-journeys they sung through the long-suffering trees to burst all round us. Of necessity we must wear our masks, but every one wore them with a difference. Beleaguered at night in a properly adjusted gas-mask, a man is at once dumb, and blind, and pre-disposed to infectious and baseless panics. It is better to face the risk of a definite and appreciated danger, and accordingly we adjusted only nose-clip and mouthpiece. There were rumours of mustard-gas, but for the moment we preferred sight to safety.

By this time the village was pandemonium, the abode of devils. The streets were blocked with fallen masonry, and everywhere the shattered houses were crumbling into rubble. The tireless thundering barrage lit the night with a flicker of yellow light-ning. Like evil spirits of infinite power and malice, the shells swept headlong through the tortured air and fanned our faces with the warm blast of their passing. A dank white fog hid the moon and held captive the stench and smoke of the bombardment.

144

Lonely sentries cowered helplessly in holes and corners among the ruins; wounded men, pale and haggard and blood-stained, staggered dizzily towards the aid-post; breathless messengers hurried by on urgent unknown errands.

About noon on the third day of our captivity the enemy opened a desultory fire on our front line. Some eight hundred yards ahead we could see the smoke of this new bombardment, and it was easy to forecast its sequel. Deterred hitherto from a frontal attack by the obstacle of the wired forest, his advance towards Chauny now allowed him to out-flank us towards the north. At dawn we might expect the long delayed climax.

VI

I can hardly tell at what precise moment desperation had its way with me. Gradually and almost
unconsciously, however, my thoughts hardened towards a resolution at all costs to escape from the
Inferno.

Over yonder, under so constant an apprehension
of death and danger, one learned to analyse motives
and call things by their proper names. Again and
again I had pondered the matter and argued it with
others, vainly trying to find solid ground beneath
shifting quicksands. Those men are greatly to be
envied who can settle once and for all the rights and
wrongs of a case, settle them and fling themselves
whole-heartedly into the battle. The doubter, the
Agnostic, the sitter on the fence, is doubly damned
in the hurly-burly. The enthusiasts on either side
despise him, and he finds himself committed to an
endless balancing of arguments. For fairness' sake,
as he thinks, he plays the part of Devil's Advocate
to every successful cause, and obstinately champions
a censured creed.

What were we all doing out there? That was the
question that hammered always in my mind. The
rhetoric of a thousand journalists will never bring
home to the civilian a tithe of what War is. The
ghastly futility of the thing; its blasphemy of God
and human nature; its contemptuous denial of
Christianity; its mechanical, cold-blooded cruelty –

only those who saw these things face to face can measure their horror. And those who know cannot share their knowledge, and a new generation grows up in ignorance.

What were we doing out there? Daily denying human nature in a vast complex of futile cruelty; plotting the destruction of strangers who, like ourselves, had not to avenge the shadow of a personal quarrel; practising the art of slaughter, and learning to smash and batter the Temple of the Holy Ghost. The wonder of modern war is, not that men are so savage, but that they are so little cruel. On the battlefield the carefully instilled lesson of ruthlessness is sometimes forgotten in remembrance of a common humanity. Instead of cracking the skull of a wounded man, Tommy and Jerry alike share with him their cigarettes and rations.

I have even heard short-sighted Atkins give way to an unmanly pacifism. 'It ought to stop. This lunacy could be ended to-day, and would be if the decision rested with us. This very day an Armistice and a Conference, and then surely the shred of sanity yet remaining in the world will secure a settlement of the quarrel. Better *any* settlement than this Golgotha.'

But the stern patriots at home took a wider view and insisted on fighting it out. 'Never will we sheathe the sword till Belgium is avenged' — as though to kill Germans miraculously revived the martyrs of Louvain. The mingled stream of prayer ascended from London and Berlin alike. Latter-day apostles were proud to baptize battleships, and in their war sermons confounded the New Testament with the Gospel of Hate. As though God would 'take sides,' as in Israel of old! Could the howling chauvinist newspapers have realized a tithe of the disgust aroused out yonder by their blood thirsty ravings, I believe even they might have learned a little wisdom. To the man in the trench the War was little more than a personal tragedy, and often he confounded friend and foe in a common humanity. Beneath the roughest rind of frightfulness lurked a shamefaced shred of pity.

It is true that the people actually doing the fighting were necessarily deprived of that high moral purpose and philosophic clarity of judgment that flower to perfection only in ease and safety. The farther you travelled from the line, the greater grew the hate, until it found a glorious culmination in fire-eating old gentlemen who nightly created hetacombs of enemies over their port wine and cigars in the Club-rooms of London and Berlin. They frothed at the mouth with warlike zeal and grew purple in the face with a noble rage. 'Would that the enemy had but one head!' And indeed the common soldier has no right to doubt the divinity of War. 'His not to reason why; his not to make reply; his but to do or die' – while the arm-chair men did the thinking for him.

Doubtless the man behind the gun did wrong to

148

doubt that all things were working together for good. Nominally he should be too busy to think, and a rum-ration is a better investment than a conscience. But he did object to the brainless ineptitudes put into his mouth by cheerful Special Correspondents, and hated above all the arm-chair critic, immune from error and the shadow of turning, wading daily through vicarious slaughter to the Kaiser's gallows-tree.

Yet I at least should have been the last to jeer at him. I had entered the Army merely because this was the line of least resistance. Towards the end of 1915 the way of the shirker was hard, and the utmost rigours of training seemed preferable to the sneers of over-righteous civilians, immune by reason of age, sex, or infirmity from what they described as 'the privilege of serving their country.' At that time I dreaded merely the discomforts of camps and billets. France and danger seemed infinitely remote.

Physical qualifications are, I suppose, justly held to be the sole test of fitness for such service. For myself, I felt as little like a soldier as any man. I hated the rough living, the exposure, the fatigue, the loss of freedom. The stifling of initiative and responsibility, the change from a name to a number, the blind, unintelligent acceptance of contradictory orders, the sinking to the level of a reliable machine that eats and drinks and sleeps, and does what it is told – I loathed them all and saw no silver lining. With only the poor consolation of knowing that I desired the pain and danger of War as little for others as for myself, I already had good reason to write myself down an arrant coward.

In the artificial surroundings of our towns there are to be found nowadays many people entirely destitute of the brave old virtue of pugnacity. On the rare occasions in their lives when force is the only remedy, they shut their eyes and telephone for the police. And now, the whole world prostrate before the God of Force, these feeble folk were expected to take a lion's share in the literal battle of life; to compete with ploughmen, coal-heavers and prize-fighters in the glorious trade of War. Small wonder they dreaded the ordeal and doubted their fitness for so terrible an emergency!

Thus numbered among the weaklings, and timidly shrinking from the bickerings of the world, I had not to cheer me even the consolation of a just quarrel. My mind was dark with doubts and questionings, and for all my muddled thinking I could not reconcile the conflicting claims of individual conscience and public interest. What had the plain citizen to do with the quarrels of diplomatists? What voice had the people in the Declaration of Wars so ably engineered by vested interests and bankrupt statesmen? Has not the individual the absolute right to steer his course independently of any guide save his own sense of right and wrong?

The Conscientious Objectors solved the problem to their own satisfaction, and for their pains went straightway to prison; true blue patriots and hot gospellers bravely tested their principles in khaki; and the doubter, shrinking alike from the finger of scorn and the growl of the guns, balanced reasons no longer and bartered future pain for present praises. He too joined the Army. And after that, the deluge!

Do you wonder that the experience of two years' service confirmed my doubts? I remembered that those at home were waiting for me, and I rated their claim higher than the Army's. It is hard to say to what extent this last argument was mere hypocrisy and the bolstering of a weak case. The drowning man clutched at every straw.

But that evening I had received a letter from home, full of hopeful looking forward and eager prayers for present safety. Enclosed were some of the first flowers of spring – primroses, early violas and a sprig of rosemary. 'There's rosemary, that's for remembrance; and there is pansies, that's for thoughts.' Such a message brought with it far more exasperation than comfort. The scent of the flowers recalled vividly the sights and sounds of home. In the intensity of my longing for the peace of the English countryside I lost all shame at leaving my companions.

VII

BY midnight on the 23rd March all save the sentries had returned to the dug-outs, and, but for an unexpected alarm, I had a couple of hours to my own devices. It was an elaborate scheme that I had planned, and I must needs carry it out with the greatest caution. A self-inflicted wound on Active Service is equivalent to desertion in the face of the enemy, and the Army has little mercy on deserters. For discipline's sake the practice must be strongly checked, and the punishment is death. More than once I had seen advertised in Routine Orders the fate of a poor wretch shot for this very crime.

Thus I was gambling for dangerously high stakes, and looking back at those things from my present sheltered harbour, I am inclined to believe that at that time I cannot have been entirely responsible for my actions. This however is doubtless a biased verdict. The court-martial would have looked at the matter very differently.

At all events the turned worm was desperate. I felt myself to be playing a lone hand — an insignificant clod of a private defying the whole organized might of the Army — but I obstinately determined to carry the thing through to the end. All that day, behind the cover of last month's *Punch*, I had pondered and weighed my chances. The scorching from a point-blank shot had proved the undoing of many, and it was necessary to find some sort of protection from the flash of the rifle. Some authorities recommended a damp sand-bag for this purpose; but such were scarce thereabouts, and a tin of bully-beef made an excellent substitute. I had discovered in the dug-out an old rusty rifle, and at first I had preferred this to my own. In my excitement I might well forget to eject the empty cartridge, and it would be a bad thing to be found with such evidence in the breach: the old rifle I could easily fling away afterwards. But later, bethinking me that so crazy a tool might well play its part too realistically by bursting in my face, I dared not run the added risk, and regretfully left it behind me.

Ostensibly I was going to fill my water-bottle at the well, where I hoped the heavy shelling would keep possible witnesses at a distance. Twice before, at a time of crisis, I had lost all my personal belongings, and I accordingly transferred from my knapsack to my pockets such necessities as a razor, two or three handkerchiefs, and the day's rations. It says much for the uncanny spell of calmness that possessed me that I was able to look so far ahead, but now that the time had come I lost my fears in a resigned and sullen self-possession.

Soon I was stumbling among the ruins of fallen houses in search of some hole or corner that would serve my purpose. I had almost decided upon a gloomy, mouldy-smelling cellar, reached with difficulty by a dozen crumbling wooden steps, when a match showed me that it was an officer's dug-out. Fortunately it was empty, and, despite so inauspicious a beginning, it did not cross my mind to accept the warning and abandon the venture. Some hundred yards away I found a cul-de-sac in a ruined house, the battered stone walls of which promised to smother the noise of the rifle.

Now that the time had come my heart was thumping uncomfortably, and I needed all my determination to persevere. Crouching in a corner of the yard, I held the rifle in my right hand, with the forefinger crooked round the trigger and my left hand a foot or so from the muzzle. Scorching at this distance would, I thought, be negligible, and the beef-tin was forgotten. Listening intently for intruders, I several times set my teeth for action, but each time hesitated and dared not take the second pressure on the trigger. All the time the shells were mocking at my delay: it would be a grim irony should they do my business for me.

At last I shut my eyes and fired almost at random. A keen burning pain shot through my left hand, and the explosion echoed deafeningly in the close-cabined space of my hiding-place. But my cowardice had brought its own punishment. A bad aim had left only a clean-cut groove in the side of the hand, palpably a bullet wound, and all was to do again. Action had given me courage, however, and, first slashing the wound with a jack-knife to hide the

154

track of the bullet, a second shot passed plumb
through the centre of the palm. A bone snapped
with a jerk and a sickening stab of pain, and I
rolled on the ground involuntarily, and gritted my
teeth to keep back the cry that might have betrayed
me.

But already I was hiding the rifle beneath a pile of
timber and listening for any sign of interruption. I
need not have feared. Who would take notice of
two rifle-shots, or who indeed would hear them
among the noises of the night? Reassured, I un-
covered my rifle and came out into the moonlight.
Almost at once I realized that I was in a tight
corner. Bad judgment had increased my danger a
hundredfold, and my hand was scorched and black
from wrist to finger-tips. It was impossible to conceal such suspicious evidence; somehow I must con-
trive to turn it to my advantage. It seemed probable that the next act of the comedy might well
be a tragedy.

Making my way back to the dug-out, and hiding
my injured hand beneath my jacket, I grumbled
to the sentry that I had left my water-bottle at the
well and must now risk the barrage again to recover
it. Also I leaned my rifle against a tree and asked
him to look after it until my return. Then away
towards the village again, and then back to the
sentry, stumbling this time and crying aloud that I
was wounded! Thus I had created a most excellent alibi: the sentry could be sure that it was not

my own rifle that had inflicted the wound. By this
time, moreover, shock had made me feel realistically
faint, and it was not deception that sent me staggering dizzily towards the aid-post. I was still deaf
from the concentrated explosion. Obviously my
story must be that I had been hit by shrapnel from
a whizz-bang.

All went well. The sentry bandaged me with a
field-dressing and showed not a shred of suspicion.
In the stretcher-bearers' dug-out explanation was
unnecessary. No doubt I looked haggard and shaken
enough, and down there in the stifling heat of the
braziers I grew so sick and giddy that men's words
came to me only as a dull and meaningless murmur.
The dressing was already soaked with blood, and
expert hands now rebandaged the wound and supported my wrist in a canvas sling. Of my equipment, I need retain nothing save gas-mask and steel
helmet. Everybody congratulated me and envied
my good fortune. I wondered what they would
have said to the truth.

Moreover I did not look forward with pleasure to
the journey to the ambulance. I had still to pass
through the barrage, and it was in vain that I pro-
tested I could find my way alone. At no time, save
during an attack, must a wounded man leave the line
unattended, and I realized with shame that my
scheming must risk the life of a stranger. It seemed,
however, that we must first report ourselves at the
Regimental Aid-post. My heart sank dejectedly.

What would the M.O. say to the blackening of my hand?

We started our journey amid a chorus of bad language and good wishes, and stumbled along the trench line to a sand-bagged cellar beneath what had once been an estaminet. There an officious sergeant insisted upon dressing my hand for the third time (and heartily I cursed his kindness), and pinned to my tunic a scrap of paper authorizing my departure from the line. I strained eyes and ears to catch the beginnings of suspicion, and even dared to ask why it was my hand had blackened. My genuine deafness, and my tale that the shell had burst beside me, carried me harmlessly through the ordeal, however, and the sergeant's sympathy extended even to cigarettes and a tot of rum.

We had next to make our way to the 'B' Company dug-outs so justly hated by the ration-parties, and again we took a roundabout course through the safer ground on the flank of the village. For a time we found little to hinder us, but the danger grew greater as we drew nearer to the houses. The flash and clamour of the barrage bewildered us; exploding shells sprinkled us with dust and chips of pavé; flying fragments sent us cowering into a ditch by the wayside. We reached shelter scared and breathless, and our proposed five minutes' breathing-space seemed likely to swell to the best part of an hour.

For my companion was enjoying our expedition

as little as I was. The route lay directly through the death-trap of the village, and we had good reason to believe that the path must be blocked with débris. The men in the dug-out did their best to make the way plain to us, but at night-time, and on such a night, I could see that they did not envy us our journey.

At last, however, we took our courage in both hands and started off at a run down the high street. Three days and nights of bombardment had changed utterly even ruined Amigny. Fallen masonry and heaps of broken bricks lay scattered over the roadway; the pavé was torn and pitted into treacherous holes and furrows. In this tumbled chaos, seen by fits and starts through the intermittent flash of the barrage, we could not distinguish the main road from side-tracks and courtyards, and we had only covered perhaps a quarter of a mile in twenty minutes when we realized that we were hopelessly astray from the proper path. For some time we groped blindly in a maze of narrow lanes and shattered mews and stables, and at last, when we emerged again in the high street not far from our starting-place, I could endure the hurly-burly no longer, and cried out desperately that 'for God's sake' we should return to shelter. There seemed nothing else to be done, and a few minutes later we were back again in the dug-out.

Restored once more by rest and a mug of tea, I was at first eager to make another attempt that night. I was convinced that the Germans would attack at dawn, and imagined myself cooped helplessly below ground while the enemy swarmed round the dug-outs. What hope then for an injured man? But the others would not hear of our going until daylight should make the path plainer. The members of a carrying-party just returned from Headquarters declared that our only hope of reaching the Buttes de Rouy lay in a masterly inactivity, and events showed that they were right.

The dug-out was occupied by the Company signallers, and ever and again messages and inquiries came to them over the wires. The man on duty was continually speaking to other little groups of men buried like ourselves in a precarious shelter from the storm. 'How are things going?' 'Heavy shelling with gas and H.E., but no signs of an attack.' 'Heard anything from "D" Company?' 'Not a word, and the wire's just gone for the third time to-night. Three men outed on repairs.' And then the voice stopped abruptly and we were left to guess what had happened.

A little group of palsied, white-faced watchers, grimy, unshaven, hollow-eyed from four days and nights that had yielded sleep only in broken snatches, gnawed by anxiety and tortured by uncertainty, what wonder if they were silent and sullen? The consciousness of disaster sapped their courage – the certainty that this present horror was merely a necessary preliminary to the real business of battle.

159

Men returning from duty outside (and some did not return) lay down silently wherever they could find a resting-place – on the floor, on the stairs, in the first cot that came to hand – and fell straightway into the sleep of exhaustion. Twitching fingers and gusty irritability discounted the feigned nonchalance of the officers. To add to their troubles, they must needs pretend that all was well.

Throughout the night I rested in a berth out of harm's way beneath the roof. Not one of the men would hear of my giving up my place, and the rations they had they shared with me. Seven o'clock brought breakfast and a loosening of tongues. The attack was still postponed and the shelling seemed set to last for ever. Refreshed by the meal, we were again ready to tempt Fortune, and climbed once more into the daylight. Warned by last night's misadventure, it was our intention to strike southwards into the Coucy Woods, where, so we were told, the shelling was far less troublesome. Tumbling breathlessly into the narrow winding trench that led thither, and passing half a dozen scattered posts of Lewis gunners, in less than ten minutes we came out upon a paved highway lined with poplars. The road ran almost exactly parallel with the line, and we only turned away from it towards the rear when well within the shelter of the forest.

And there, as by enchantment, we escaped from the dust and roar of the bombardment into another world – the old familiar world of trees and fields

160

and sunshine. Behind us lay the Abomination of
Desolation – a land of scorched and cratered meadows, of shattered riven hedgerows, and homes
abandoned and made desolate. The smoke and reek
of War hung over it; the fair face of the earth was
warped and cankered in a long-drawn agony. Here
the sun shone blithely from a sky of forget-me-not
blue, the trees and fields were whole and fair, the
noise of the guns lay behind us like a dying storm.
For the first time for four long days and nights we
could rest, and linger by the way, and watch the
shadow of the clouds upon the meadows.

Our way wound through woods full of the frag-
rance of damp leaves by narrow paths of mingled
shade and sunshine. Fragile nodding anemones and
the yellow stars of Wordsworth's celandines smiled
bravely at the sun. The 'lambs' tails' hung in
clusters from the hazel-bushes, and the honey-
scented flowers of the palm were packed in mus-
tard-yellow clusters upon tough leafless branches.
Larks sang high above the tree-tops. 'The lowest
boughs and the brushwood sheaf round the elm-
tree bole were in tiny leaf.' But this gentle joy of
Nature at Spring's birth-time men were too busy
to see. Other and more important duties distracted
their attention.

Beyond the forest our path lay over meadows
among the tangled wire of the Battle Area. But the
trenches were tenantless and the gun emplace-
ments empty save for shining stacks of abandoned

shells. High overhead beyond the river floated a German observation-balloon in ominous security.

We met not a soul between the Coucy Woods and the twin hummocks of the Buttes de Rouy, where Headquarters had long been raked by an obstinate bombardment. For there all manner of work and traffic had once found shelter, and in the lea of the hills, beneath an elaborate camouflage of painted canvas and green netting, had gathered a busy camp of field-kitchens, ammunition dumps, horse-lines, howitzer batteries, and all the rag-tag and bobtail of the sector. But now the market-place was empty, and the booths and huts lay scattered in ruins. The guns and the transport-limbers had withdrawn towards the river. The canteen beside the road had been wrecked by a shell. The long narrow tunnels that honeycombed the hills were empty save for a group of signallers and the staff of the Regimental Aid-post.

But I had now to face perhaps the greatest risk of the journey. In broad daylight, and among men no longer distracted by the urgency of danger, deception would be far more difficult. Another examination might well prove my undoing, but the stretcher-bearer had heard my story, and I dared not abandon the myth of the whizz-bang. An unexpected piece of good fortune solved the problem, however. The M.O. was most fortunately asleep, and our explanation that the wound had already been dressed and ticketed was an excuse for the

162

tired orderly to pass me without further formality into a kind of waiting-room, where I had only to rest and smoke and hope for an early ambulance.

Here I saw the last of my companion, who waited only for a drink of tea before beginning his long trudge back to Amigny. I heard later that he was killed that same day by shrapnel.

VIII

As I lay smoking peacefully in the straw-lined bunk, I remember saying to myself that at all events I had won the first round. My chief feeling for the moment was one of pride that I had been able so far to evade the strong hand of the law, and I redoubled my determination to cheat it to the end.

The ambulance was long delayed, and I passed the time plotting and planning my future movements. Suddenly I remembered a capital error. It was an absurdly trivial matter, but much might turn upon it. Had I got rid of my empty cartridge? For the life of me I could not remember ejecting it. I foresaw the examination of my rifle – almost certainly blood-stained. How did the marks come there if I had left it behind me before I was wounded? And what was the explanation of the empty case? For the moment I could think of no better answer to the first question than blank ignorance. Perhaps I had leaned against the rifle on my return to the dug-out. As for the empty cartridge, most opportunely I remembered the rumour of attack two hours before midnight. The battalion in the front line had opened rifle-fire on what proved afterwards to have been merely a German patrol. Stray shots fired in retaliation had whizzed past our ears in the second line, and, carried away by excitement, I had (obviously) fired in return and forgotten to eject the cartridge.

This was a weak enough defence, but I could think of nothing better. Above all I must keep to my tale of shrapnel so long as I remained in the company of those who knew that no hand-to-hand fighting had yet taken place on the sector; but at the first opportunity I was determined to substitute the far more plausible story of a wound received point-blank.

Already I was beginning to pay the price of my treachery. The shame of this petty scheming and a growing fear of discovery were an unforeseen punishment. Free from the distractions of action and danger, I grew fearful and despondent. I had bartered self-respect for safety.

At ten o'clock the ambulance was still to seek, and my impatience grew rapidly towards panic. At all costs I must escape from the neighbourhood of my own battalion. At any moment I might be face to face with discovery.

Thus goaded, I asked leave to join some men of the R.A.M.C. who were on the point of returning from the aid-post to the advanced dressing-station at Sinceny. Permission was readily given, but an unexpected difficulty delayed us.

The only other casualty in the dug-out was a shell-shocked artilleryman – a timid, shrinking little man with wandering, lack-lustre eyes and a livid yellow face above a limp black moustache. For some time it was impossible to rouse him. To all questions he gave but one answer: 'Anything so long as I get away from those guns!' He repeated these words continually in an expressionless, whispering monotone, and, when at last with shuffling, dragging footsteps the poor fellow made shift to accompany us, we had not covered fifty yards before he collapsed in a ditch by the wayside. A drink of water revived him, but it was clear that he must return to the aid-post. We tried in vain to make him understand that an ambulance would soon be carrying him to safety. Our words meant nothing to him, and, gazing at vacancy with clouded eyes that still saw horrors to us invisible, he fell once more to the recital of his litany, and did not even know that we were leaving him.

'Coal-boxes' were bursting behind us over the Buttes, and to escape them we steered a zigzag course over the meadows. These were the last fringe of danger, however, and presently we returned to the road for the sake of better going. Out here on the grassy slopes that skirted the forest we could see neither man nor horse nor gun. The wide misty landscape was empty; a darting biplane (whether friend or foe we knew not) was the only thing that seemed alive. But away across the valley the rattle of machine-guns waxed and waned capriciously, and tall columns of dun-coloured smoke marked the sites of burning villages.

At a bend in the road, where all traffic by day must make a detour into the fields to avoid hostile observation, we came suddenly upon a French mitrailleuse mounted upon a lorry, its outlines hidden by a tangle of fir-branches. The gunners in their smart blue uniforms grinned cheerfully at us as we passed, but a British military policeman at the cross-roads was less amiable. Had he but known it, he had good reason for his suspicions; but my ticket was not to be denied, and he opened for us the last barrier to safety. Outwardly I was for-lorn enough, but I laughed in my sleeve.

Sinceny village was strongly garrisoned by the French. Officers were staring through field-glasses towards the enigma beyond the river; the smoke of field-kitchens curled lazily among the ruined houses; men were digging trenches behind the shelter of a line of hedges.

In a house less shattered than most we found the Advanced Dressing-station, already three parts empty, and the officer in charge fussing desper-ately. He had, perhaps, reason for his impatience. The Y.M.C.A. hut over the way was forlorn and deserted; Brigade Headquarters had vanished; canteen and post offce alike had folded their tents. But the major did not sufficiently conceal his anxiety, and fumed and shouted until even his own men laughed at him. He was one of those large pink men, clean-shaven and immaculate, who do themselves well under all circumstances, and he seemed by no means to appreciate so sudden and urgent a catastrophe.

In this excitement of departure I once again

167

avoided examination, but secured in exchange for my roughly scribbled ticket an official Field Casualty Card. Medical stores, furniture and kit were dumped into waiting lorries, and two motor-ambulances just sufficed to contain the staff and perhaps a score of casualties. In less than half an hour the dressing-station was empty.

We had only travelled as far as the Chauny high road, however, when we were stopped by a man badly wounded in arm and shoulder. Where he came from no one knew, but his plight was obviously desperate. Unfortunately there was not an inch of room in any of the ambulances, and no one seemed anxious to leave their shelter. Not a man of the Royal Army Medical Corps could be spared from duty, and there was therefore only one way out of the difficulty. Were any of the patients able to walk?

This was an invidious and doubtful question. Two of the men were bad cases of shell-shock. Pale beneath a mask of grime, and with eyes that blinked and wandered, not a muscle in their bodies but quivered and trembled convulsively. Head and limbs were racked by a merciless palsy, and one of them who was trying to smoke a cigarette could hold it neither in his mouth nor his fingers. The elder of the two, stuttering and stammering horribly, told me how he had been sitting on the ground with his back against the trunk of an apple tree. A shell hit the base of the tree, and the explosion flung him ten yards across the orchard. He re-covered consciousness as we saw him – deaf and dazed and twitching.

The other men were variously afflicted. Two had lost an arm and one a leg. Another, his jaw smashed by shrapnel into a pulp of flesh and bone, groaned and grunted like a wild beast in a hopeless effort to speak. Blood and saliva oozed in a red foam from the mouth of a man shot through the lung. On one of the cots lay a poor fellow whose left leg, snapped at the ankle, projected from a swathe of bandages as a splinter of bone stained black with iodine.

All were manifestly worse off than I – all, that is, save a smiling poilu who discreetly knew no Eng-lish – and, to the delight of the palpitating major, I volunteered to leave the convoy and make my own way to the field-ambulance at Quirczy. If this should seem inconsistent with my late conduct, I can only suggest that I had no quarrel with fellow-victims.

From Sinceny to Quirczy is about six kilometres, and it took me three hours to cover them. My gas-mask I had left behind at the dressing-station, but I retained my shrapnel helmet as a sunshade. It was a wretched enough journey, and by three o'clock, when I reached the field-ambulance, I was ready to drink from a puddle and sleep in a ditch.

Mounted military police were warning every one

to get away to the rear, and spread panic by insisting that certain dull and loaded detonations near at hand marked the demolition of the Chauny bridges. Once a captain of machine-gunners emerged from the shelter of a hedge and questioned me eagerly. Where was the line, and where were the Huns? Naturally I could tell him nothing save that the Germans had so far delivered no attack on this side of the river.

Everywhere the road was blocked with artillery, and even the 'Archies' were pausing only to fire half a dozen rounds by the wayside. Horses, men, guns and transport were streaming towards the west, packed more and more closely as they left the line farther behind them. The paraphernalia of two armies mingled pell-mell together. French infantry in horizon-blue straggled over the road, overburdened by their mountainous equipment; a string of cantankerous mules pressed hard upon a battery of 'seventy-fives'; and close on their heels came a jumble of British field-kitchens, transport-wagons, camouflaged eighteen-pounders, ambulances, staff-cars, and innumerable lorries.

It was a sunny, cloudless afternoon. The dust powdered the clothes of the men, and sweat drew shining muddy channels on their faces. The air was heavy with the stench of men and mules and petrol. Sometimes the men sang, and sometimes they swore; but always they gave me a friendly nod, and more than once a priceless Woodbine. 'Cheerio, chum. Caught one?' A 'walking-wounded' is privileged indeed. For the moment he is his own master, and concerned with nothing except his own safety. Thus he is in some sort a care-free spectator, and, cheered by the knowledge that he is leaving all this maddened welter behind him, he is encouraged to notice details that at any other time would pass unheeded and unseen.

Despite persistent rumours to the contrary, the Oise bridges at Chauny were still intact, and the sergeant of Engineers in charge of the demolition-party there gave me from his water-bottle the finest draught of red wine that ever gladdened the heart of man. I am thus hyperbolical deliberately, for mere words were inadequate to thank him. This good Samaritan, like a thousand others we met in France, helped me and passed on, and stayed not for gratitude. We never saw them again, and whether they lived or died we knew not.

Divisional Headquarters was evacuating Quirczy, and the field-ambulance, where not long ago I had spent a lazy week of convalescence, was preparing to follow it. When last I saw it the orderly activities of a 'forward area' seemed set to run for ever, but now nothing but was out of joint. In the dismantled reception-room a solitary staff-corporal examined my hand, washed and rebandaged the wound, and gave me the inevitable injection against lock-jaw. Now that I had escaped from the battalion I could safely assert that my trouble was a point-blank bullet-wound. Hence the scorching. 'I can see you've been mixed up with them,' said the corporal with an air of admiration, but my sense of the humour of the occasion was sadly blunted by shame.

In a marquee near at hand three men, with but two useful hands between them, managed to cut up some hunks of stale bread, and drank cold tea from a sooty dixie. While we were eating, a wandering sergeant amused us with cheerful conversation. 'This ambulance has been a ruddy shambles since the morning of the 21st. Hardly a man of us has had a wink of sleep for three days. Now we're off somewhere towards Noyon, but God knows where we're going. You chaps had better hop into anything you can find on wheels. The Jerries'll be here in an hour or two, and if you don't look slippy you'll catch another bumping.'

This was sufficiently explicit. We made haste to claim a place in a waiting ambulance, and so rode back another fifteen kilometres along roads dusty with a variegated traffic to the Casualty Clearing-station at Noyon. In the fields men were digging shallow emergency-trenches and mounting machine-guns behind the hedges. Civilians reappeared on the roads and, as we drew nearer to Noyon, we came upon parties of peasants in carts and farm-wagons, crouching wretchedly among bales and crates and boxes that held all that they had been able to save from homes suddenly aban-

doned. Old women were pushing along the dusty
road wheelbarrows and mailcarts piled high with
bundles, toiling forward slowly and hopelessly,
while the tears ran down their faces. These were
adventurous souls who had returned to their ruined
villages after the great German retreat of 1917. No
sooner had they settled themselves to the long task
of restoration than the new blow fell, and once
again they must abandon everything and trust to
the charity of strangers.

It was no wonder that they looked sourly on us –
the Allies who seemed to have failed them. The bad
news had spread like the shadow of black clouds,
and roused the countryside. 'English no bon,'
yapped the emigrants as we passed them, and it
was hard to blame their anger. Everywhere was the
same atmosphere of incredulous anxiety. Had all our
boastings come to this? On the faces of a group of
staff-officers I thought I saw an expression of shamefaced rage – as though they suspected us of cursing
their fine linen, and the strategy that had led to a
débâcle.

The clearing-station at Noyon lay, of course, close
to the railway, and thither the wounded had filtered
by a hundred streams. Built originally by the
French, the place was made up of some dozens of
wooden huts and large canvas marquees, with wood-
paved paths between them and lawns and flower-
beds beside the paths. A throng of men crowded
every corner, and order and discipline had long

173

since vanished. In such a hurly-burly there could be no systematic examination of new-comers, and only desperate cases – mangled shreds and patches of men – were admitted to wards already paved with stretchers. There was a rumour of bread and tea in a canteen beside the railway, but such was the shouting and turmoil round the entrance that it seemed hopeless to join in the struggle. We threw our 'tin-hats' into a huge growing dump by the wayside and waited with what patience we might for the train to the base. Always the crowd was growing larger: always the bearers were carrying to the mortuary something hidden from sight beneath a blanket.

But it did us good to see the Sisters. To keep a stiff upper lip in such surroundings; to force a smile when tears long to come; to treat grown men tenderly, as a mother treats her baby; to persevere under the utmost pressure of emergency – what does it cost to do these things? One of the nurses told me that a hospital ward tried to breaking-point her trust in God, while it strengthened immeasurably her faith in man. Such sufferings borne in grim, tight-lipped silence or with quaint facetiousness! The heroism of the ordinary man! The persistence of courage against all odds! Yet it was man that inflicted these torments, and one at least of that unhappy multitude could claim no share in their praise. But even to him the sight of these brave women carried a message from a better world, and from the moment he set eyes on them he realized again the meaning of home and England.

We had been promised a train by eight o'clock; but nine came, and ten, and eleven, and still not a sign of it! Long before dark we were wild with impatience; the aimless lounging, the flying rumours and bartered tales of horror exasperated us to desperation. A story gained ground that the Germans were within an hour's march of the town, and as dusk grew to darkness, the men crowded round the officers' quarters and shouted for ambulances as an alternative to trekking. Military police were powerless to check them, for not even the 'red-caps' could do anything drastic to wounded men.

It was a weird scene in the moonlight (for not a lamp could be lighted for fear of aeroplanes) where some thousands of wanderers lay scattered in every stage of dirt and rags and maiming. Excitement kept them garrulous and lurid yarns of adventure inflamed their fears. An uncontrollable restlessness sent them prying and peering into corners, feverishly wandering and looking for they knew not what. Sometimes they sought rest on stretchers or tumbled piles of blankets, but always the rumour of a train disturbed them, and they dared not sleep lest they should lose their chance of safety. Several poor fellows only partially crippled were crawling and hopping desperately in a crowd which seemed inclined rather to hinder than to help them.

175

For we were strained to the last pitch of endurance: nerves were on edge and tempers raw to distraction. All that evening I heard sounding in my ears the hiss and roar of the barrage. We were light-headed with anxiety and the fever of wounds, and the sleep that alone could cure us seemed banished from the world.

Several times we wandered aimlessly to the railway station, where a scared crowd of civilians clamoured impotently for trains and stared at us wide-eyed as at wild beasts from a menagerie. (And they had cause.) At the Y.M.C.A. hut, still bravely open, and at several estaminets we sought in vain for food and drink. Stocks were everywhere exhausted, and all men concerned chiefly with dread of to-morrow. Their fears were well-founded, for next morning the Germans captured the town and seized the clearing-station for billets.

It was long after midnight when our train at last arrived. For more than an hour there had been a noise of shunting in the distance, and we were not surprised to find that the journey was to be made in cattle-trucks. The last Red Cross train, crowded with stretcher-cases, had left soon after nine o'clock, and no other transport was available. Already many of the seriously wounded had been evacuated in wagons and lorries. To enjoin haste a few shells fell haphazard on the town.

Yet even now we must resign ourselves to further waiting. We were marshalled in a long line by the rail-side, and made our way slowly down the length of the train, thirty men clambering into each truck. And then there followed an intolerable and inexplicable delay. For two more hours we were kept in gusty impatience outside the station, and then, in the small hours of the morning, at last began our journey to the sea. The moon had vanished and the closed trucks were as black as a cave at midnight, but we were leaving behind us the welter of the line, and looked eagerly forward to to-morrow.

Thirty men in a French cattle-truck without their equipment can rest in comparative comfort. Forms or seats there were none, but we sorted ourselves as best we could in the darkness into two long lines on either side of the wagon, our feet meeting in the middle. Few had overcoats or ground-sheets, and in our anxiety we had left the blankets behind us. By hugging together in pairs we made shift to keep almost warm, however, and a philanthropist even sought to cheer us with a mouth-organ. There were no rations and, above all, no cigarettes, so that his cheerfulness was the more praiseworthy.

The journey to the Base took fourteen hours. Most of the men in my truck were only slightly injured, and the jolting of the train was thus to them no more than annoying: those with body-wounds were, I imagine, less happy. Sleeping in broken snatches, we somehow tossed and turned and swore our way through the five hours of darkness, and, when day broke, pulled back the sliding doors

to find the train grinding slowly through an unfamiliar landscape of wide flat cornlands. The sunlight
did not flatter us. The sorry-looking crew of scarecrows in the wagon were dirty and ragged and
unshaven, with dark rings under their eyes and the
wolfish ill-temper of men tried wellnigh past endurance. The truck stank horribly of blood and
dirt and the air was rank with fetid exhalations.

Early in the morning we halted at a small country
town, where ladies of the French Red Cross Service
brought out to us mugs of steaming café-cognac.
The warm drink cheered us mightily, but beyond
a shamefaced 'Merci' and 'Très bien' we could do
little to show our gratitude. The Sisters, I thought,
showed their courage in approaching the menagerie
thus fearlessly.

While we waited there passed us a French Division 'going up the line,' and with them also our
conversation was sadly limited. Loudly proclaim-
ing the obvious, we shouted to them that we were
'blessé à la ligne,' and they replied with the familiar
shibboleths of 'Sale boche' and 'C'est la guerre.'
We understood one another well enough, however,
and seemed to find an irrational pleasure in the
meeting. This must have been one of the Divisions
that filled the gap between Amiens and Soissons,
and a few hours later they were doubtless in desperate action.

Soon after noon we drew up at a siding beside
a Y.M.C.A. hut and a dressing-station. Mugs of

hot tea, hunks of bread, jam, bully-beef, cigarettes, field-cards — I cannot hope to convey to you the dizzy joy we found in them. We wolfed the food unashamed like starving animals, and lit our Woodbines with a fearful joy. The orderlies bandaged afresh those men whose wounds were bleeding from the jolting of the train, and cheered us with tales of the flesh-pots of hospital. As we left behind us the stark horrors of the line, we insensibly invested ourselves with something of the traditional gaiety of the wounded Tommy. We could hardly do otherwise: we only now began to realize the extent of our good fortune.

We reached Rouen about five o'clock, but waiting ambulances shattered our hope of Blighty. Ten minutes later we were in hospital, but not the calm haven of our dreams. At this time the Base hospitals were hopelessly congested by the sudden pressure of casualties. An ever-rising tide submerged them, and train succeeded train by day and night. The huts and tents were full to overflowing, and convoys leaving daily for England did little to relieve them. Each empty bed had three men to fill it, and the routine of the place had gone all to pieces. The orderlies told me that since the beginning of the German offensive they had been working for twenty hours a day. Baths and meals and dressings were dispensed haphazard: there was no one to give orders, and for the most part we were left to our own devices.

179

The throng in the steaming bath-house was so
great that it was hard to find even standing-room.
My left hand was of course useless, and thus dis-
abled I tangled myself hopelessly in towels and clothing. Seen through the drifting clouds of steam, the
crowded naked bodies of the men, and their halt-
ing, clumsy, fettered movements, made an excellent
illustration for a canto of the *Inferno*. But an hour
later we forgot all our troubles in the breathless
luxuries of clean sheets, fresh linen and a soft
mattress. Our shelter was a draughty and ill-lit
marquee, but it seemed to us a palace. We were
asleep almost before we were in bed.

But that evening I had been warned for an operation, and about midnight my sleep was roughly
broken: 'Come along, chum, get a move on. You're
for the butcher's shop.' They do not believe in
euphemism in a military hospital. Huddling on
trousers and tunic, I groped my way down dark
passages to the theatre and resigned myself to an
hour's meditation in the lobby. The floor was
paved with stretchers, and those of us who could
walk stepped gingerly over them to a bench in the
corner. It was a dreary ordeal. Some of the men on
the stretchers were in such agony that they could
not keep still or silent for a single moment. The
big swing-doors leading to the theatre opened and
shut continually, and within we caught sight of
red-stained horrors lying side by side upon the
tables. The reek of ether and chloroform clogged

the air, and through the doors came the sound of hoarse, stertorous breathing, broken sometimes by sudden strident shrieks that set us asking anxious questions. 'Do they always give chloroform?' 'Oh yes; the chap that's making that row doesn't know what's happening to him.' But we would have been glad of stronger confirmation.

There were six tables in the theatre, and the less serious cases were dealt with on stretchers on the floor. From an unconscious man on one of the nearer tables came a shrill, tireless, monotonous yelling, and not far away four orderlies were holding down another who was fighting desperately against the anæsthetic. Pale, tired-looking doctors examined me; the sweetish scent of ether filled my nostrils; somewhere inside my head a wheel began to spin dizzily; the wheel became confused with the beating of a drum; the drum beat more and more softly, and I floated away into a sea of darkness and silence, to awake, sick and giddy, in the familiar gloom of the marquee. To the doctors I had repeated my story that the wound was from a bullet fired point-blank, but my dread was that I should blab my secret under the anæsthetic. My fears were once more groundless, however. The orderlies assured me that I had opened my mouth only in harmless and normal blasphemy.

In the morning the Sister recommended me to get my papers from the theatre and to see the officer in charge of the ward with a view to getting 'marked for Blighty.' Such freedom of action was unprecedented in my experience, but this was no time for diffidence. I interviewed a truculent major in the receiving-room, satisfied him that I was fit to travel, and emerged triumphantly bearing papers marked in red ink with the magic 'E.' Fortune favours the coward.

Two days later I was officially warned for England. (In the Army you are 'warned' for everything – coal-fatigues, bombing raids, England, France, and your 'ticket.') In a delicious flutter of excitement, I changed once again from hospital-blue to khaki, claimed my papers in the popular waterproof envelope, and travelled by ambulance with an exulting multitude to Rouen station. There we found a string of cattle-trucks luxuriously fitted with benches (obviously a leave train), received rations of bread, butter, beef and biscuits, and were told that our destination was Le Havre.

This was sufficient to convert even the most obstinate pessimists, and our failure to recognize the familiar route through Barentin and Yvetot worried us not at all. But our high hopes were premature. In the midst of an animated discussion of the relative merits of Leeds and London we fell to earth abruptly in the unexpected terminus of Trouville-sur-Mer, a dozen miles from Havre on the other side of the Seine estuary. Obviously this was no port for Blighty, and we besieged the staff of the train for explanations. The latter at first professed complete ignorance, and then told us that our present position was due to a misunder-standing; in half an hour we should be returning to Le Havre by way of Rouen. This sounded too fantastic even for Army transport; but we clutched eagerly at any straw, and did our best to believe them. In the light of after-events, I believe they were merely afraid to tell us the unwelcome truth.

But this meagre thread of hope soon snapped. On a range of hills towards the west was a long line of buildings, crowned by a Red Cross flag. We could not help realizing that this was a large Base hospital, and after two hours' further delay the train backed out of the station and took a branch line towards the foot of the hills. In a few minutes it turned remorselessly into a siding, and we received orders to detrain.

There were waiting for us some dozens of open trucks fitted with seats in the manner of a switch-back at a fair. A narrow-gauge railway climbed the hill-side in a series of zigzags, and carried us rapidly through fields of young corn and budding woodland. Wide views opened inland towards the south, but we were in no mood to appreciate them. We felt that we had been 'sold,' and it exasperated us to be treated like children who must do as they are told without the saving grace of reasons.

The engineers on the light railway confirmed our fears. There were no less than four hospitals at Trouville, and they laughed at our hopes of Blighty.

Thousands had passed that way with a similar story. A few of the men swore whole-heartedly, but most were sullenly silent: the high hopes of the morning had turned to dust and ashes.

And that was the end of our dreams. Instead of an English hospital, a noisy Convalescent Camp in France, with trestle-beds, rough food, and all the fatigues and discomforts that went with them! The rush of reinforcements from England had cut down the available transport, and we were marooned at Trouville that we might not clog the lines of communication. But we found it difficult to look at the matter thus dispassionately, and after a scrambling half-hearted meal in the crowded mess-room, crept sullenly to our allotted huts and made shift to forget our troubles in sleep. For myself, I was not far from tears.

Bᴜᴛ worse was to follow. After twenty-four hours
in Camp a great number of the more obviously
ill and helpless were transferred to hospital, myself
among them. A week later the walking wounded
were removed to a new and partially completed
colony that resembled nothing so much as a builder's
yard. There was little to see but mud and cement,
timber and ironwork; and everywhere stood the
gaunt skeletons of huts and bungalows. An army of
German prisoners was at work there, but for many
weeks we lived in a limbo of muddle and makeshift. The ward at first contained only beds, bedding, and empty lockers, with a defective anthra-
cite stove and three hurricane lamps. Outside, a
sea of mud ended only at the doorway.

These discouraging surroundings underlined our
original disappointment and sunk us in an apathy
of pessimism. I in particular had creeping fears to
keep me company. We had chummed together on
the journey in the usual Army way, but birds of
passage like ourselves could never stay long together.
In each hospital we found new neighbours. The
man who shared your rations to-day, to-morrow you
lost for ever.

Those long lonely weeks at Trouville were a
penance to me. I was haunted by the fear of discovery, and suffered almost the remorse of a mur-
derer. Terrified by my dread of the death-penalty,

night after night I dreamed that the worst had befallen me. I pictured to myself the firing-party and the word of command; the crash of the volley and 'the nothing all things end in.' Again and again I recalled the details of that eventful evening, and shrank again from the shock of the bullet. The rifle, the scorching of the wound, the sound of the shots, the chance of an eavesdropper – I brooded miserably over the most sinister possibilities and tried to fashion a line of defence against every shred of evidence. Or should I admit the fact, but insist on an accident? Or would it be best to confess and ask for mercy? Wrapped all day in this obstinate cloak of introspection, I feared above all to betray myself by words shouted in the morbid dreams from which I awoke trembling and dreading the beginnings of madness. I remembered that the others were still there in the line, doing their duty that I might live in safety. Thus despising myself, I almost grew to envy what I now called their happiness. The healthy thoughts of the past seemed banished for ever.

Towards the end of the third week the Sister told me that 'an inquiry' had been made about me, and for the moment I thought that the murder was out – that the message came from the battalion. 'What's the matter with you, chum? You're as white as a sheet,' said somebody; and I muttered some story of a headache and smoked cigarettes furiously. But a guilty conscience had betrayed me for nothing.

A telegram had come from home, and my fears of a court-martial were groundless.

This indeed was the ebb-tide of my courage, and gradually, as the days passed without catastrophe, I recovered my confidence and attained almost to cheerfulness. Books were my salvation and helped me to forget. The memory of the crime grew blurred with distance, and time dulled its shame.

For nearly three months I remained at Trouville, in different wards and under different forms of treatment. At first I watched carefully the faces of nurses and doctors for the first hint of suspicion; but the slow cleaning of my scorched hand washed away the blackest evidence, and at last I told myself that I had definitely won the game. But it was still necessary to walk carefully. As soon as the wound had healed I volunteered for light duty with the Hospital Police, and so contrived to waste three weeks without massage. By this means I might evade a complete recovery, and with normal luck make a bid for a medical board, a low category, and a job at the Base.

But my good fortune went further, and at an hour's notice I was warned for an English convoy. In mid-June I left France for good, and in due time the Army. Behold me now with a War Gratuity and a Pension, Gold Stripes and Service Chevrons, the reputation of a man who has done his bit, and the unconsciously ironical gratitude of strangers!

And was it, after all, worth while to barter self-

respect for safety? Often I wish I had risked everything and taken my chance with the others. Often
I tell myself that it was on the knees of the Gods
whether in that event I should have emerged at all
from the struggle; that death on a battlefield is
merely the crowning absurdity to a life of folly;
that self-preservation is no crime. Perhaps it is th'
knowledge of the thousands who evaded so successfully the horrors of the War – profited by them
rather – that reconciles me most of all to my own
weakness. There is a grim humour in the voluble
explanations of those who somehow failed to bear
the burden.

But though I protest until my tongue cleave to
the roof of my mouth, the coward is a coward still,
and nothing can exonerate him. I hoped only to
give you some notion of what war may mean to a
weakling. At least I have hidden nothing. What
you think of me I shall never know.

X

For the train had reached Exeter, and my companion vanished so abruptly that I had not even time to wish him farewell. I have never seen him since, and indeed I feel sure that it was only to a stranger that he could have made confession. To all of us in its season there comes the desire to tear aside the veils of reticence: it so happened that the time and the occasion were favourable to me. The unknown's conduct I dare not judge. His story must speak for itself.